DARK PRINCE

AN AGE GAP, FORCED MARRIAGE ROMANCE

K.C. CROWNE

DESCRIPTION

"Be a good girl and do as you're told,"
His baritone voice thunders through the hall.

Attending a sinister party with my stepmother...
The knowing eyes of strangers send chills down my spine.
Suddenly, a horrifying truth dawns on me: this isn't just ***any*** party.
It's my **GOD D*MN** wedding night.
Towering above me, a foot and a half taller...
Lukyan Ivanov.
Coldhearted killer. Feared by all. Including me.
My stepmother sold my soul to the devil himself to repay her debts.
My plan: escape.
But a plot twist stops me dead in my tracks.
I get pregnant with Lukyan's child,
And he transforms into someone entirely new:
A devoted husband who'll unleash hell to protect his family.

Readers note: This is full-length standalone, Russian mafia/bratva, forced marriage, age-gap romance in the bestselling Silver Fox Daddies series. K.C. Crowne is an Amazon Top 6 Bestseller and International Bestselling Author.

CHAPTER 1

MAURA

"You're quite the vision tonight. A real shame your father isn't here to see this." The man says. His gaze lingering on my neckline for an uncomfortably long time.

I'm confused by his choice of words.

"To see what, *exactly*?"

As he walks away, he throws a cryptic comment over his shoulder. "Enjoy the big evening, Maura. It'll be one to remember." Sean O'Donnell is a low level mob boss closely tied with the Irish underworld.

The world I was born into.

His strange words hang in the air, heavy with an unspoken meaning that sends a shiver down my spine.

As I stand in the center of the grand ballroom, the emerald green of my gown in stark contrast to the sea of dark suits. The dress—though stunning with its fitted bodice and flowing skirt—feels like a costume in this world of shadows, sinister glares, and hushed threats.

The silk clings to my curves, a bold choice my stepmother insisted upon, saying it was time I looked the part of Irish mafia royalty—whatever *that* means.

The grandeur of the ballroom is overwhelming, with high ceilings adorned with elaborate chandeliers that cast a soft, golden glow over the crowd. Mob bosses and their entourages move through the space, their conversations a low hum beneath the gentle sounds coming from the string quartet playing in the corner.

The air is thick with the scent of expensive cologne and the subtle hint of danger that always seems to accompany gatherings like this. I stand near a tall, arched window, admiring the night sky, wondering what is beyond. I take a small sip from the crystal flute in my hand, the champagne cool and crisp on my tongue. I can't help but feel out of place despite the elegance of my gown and the way it complements the grandeur around me.

As I look about, I realize my stepmother never actually told me why this party is being held. There's usually a reason for these gatherings: a celebration, an announcement, a ceremony. But no reason for tonight's festivities was given.

What's more unsettling is the way people keep staring.

Not the usual looks I've grown accustomed to, those lingering, often lecherous stares from men who see me as nothing more than a potential trophy. No, these looks are different—curious, speculative, almost wary.

As if they know something I don't.

It sets my nerves on edge.

I'm about to take another sip of my champagne when I spot my stepmother. She moves through the crowd with a grace that belies her true nature, her blonde hair styled perfectly, her blue eyes scanning the room like a predator assessing its territory. She's dressed in a perfectly tailored evening gown with a low cut neckline. The fabric is a deep navy that contrasts sharply with her fair skin. Her jewelry—always expensive yet understated—catches the light as she moves. There's a warm, almost charming smile on her lips, but her eyes remain cold and calculating.

As she approaches me, her smile widens.

Clearly forced.

"Maura, darling, you look lovely tonight," she says, her voice dripping with a sweetness that I've learned to distrust.

I nod politely. "Thank you, Sharon. That's very kind. I was just wondering what the occasion is for tonight's gathering?"

"Sharon...," she says, clicking her tongue and shaking her head. "How many times do I have to remind you to call me mom?"

It takes all my self-control not to roll my eyes.

She's not my mother.

The woman doesn't have a maternal bone in her body.

"About the party, can you please clue me in?" I say changing the subject.

"Oh, you'll find out soon enough," she replies cryptically, her gaze sweeping over the room before settling back on me. "Just enjoy the gathering, Maura. After all, it's not every day we have such a... special event."

I narrow my eyes at Sharon's response. The patience for such games has long since left me. "I don't appreciate the mystery, Sharon," I say, my voice firm.

Sharon's smile falters slightly, but she quickly regains her composure. Her eyes gleam with a hint of triumph as she leans in closer. "Very well, Maura. I suppose now's as good a time as any for you to find out. The reason for tonight's celebration is quite simple—you're getting married."

Her words hit me like a physical blow. For a moment, I'm convinced I've misheard what she said. "Married?" I echo, my voice barely above a whisper. "That's impossible."

"Trust me, it's very possible," Sharon replies, her tone smug. "It's all been arranged. You'll meet your fiancé soon enough."

The room spins around me, the faces of the mobsters blurring into a mass of indistinct figures. "This is insane," I protest, anger flaring up inside me. "What do you mean I'm getting married?"

"Married. You know—husband, wife, perhaps some kids."

I feel like I'm in the middle of a sick prank, but Sharon's calculating look makes it clear she's not joking around.

"You can't just decide my life for me. I'm not some pawn in your games."

But Sharon's smile only widens, like a predator baring its teeth. "My dear, you'll find that I certainly can make decisions for you, and I have. And you are my pawn."

I turn on my heel, my heart pounding in my chest. I need to get out of there, away from this marriage madness. Pushing through the crowd, I focus only on reaching the exit and on escaping this nightmare.

In my haste, I collide with a solid wall of muscle. Stumbling back, I find myself staring up into the face of Rory Murphy, Sharon's personal bodyguard. He's a towering figure with weathered features that silently tell the tale of a lifetime spent in the underworld of the Irish mafia. His burly frame blocks out the rest of the room.

I look down at his huge, calloused hands, forced to recall the bruises they left on my body whenever Sharon ordered him to rough me up, always careful to avoid my face. The memories of those encounters make me shiver, a mix of fear and resentment boiling inside me.

As I attempt to make my escape, Rory's hand clamps down on my arm with an iron grip. "Let go of me! "I scream, struggling against his hold, but it's like trying to move a mountain.

My protests seem to fall on deaf ears among the party attendees. Their amusement is evident in their smirks and raised eyebrows as they watch my futile attempts to free myself.

Rory, unphased by my resistance, steers me back toward Sharon, who stands watching the spectacle with cold satisfaction. "You see, Maura," she says as I'm brought before her, "you really don't have a choice in this. Your father's gone, and I'm in charge now."

"You have no right to speak of him," I spit back at her, my voice laced with venom.

As Rory's firm grip prevents any escape, Sharon leans in, her voice dripping with malice. "You shouldn't act so high and mighty. After all, I've done more than just speak your father's name," she sneers, her eyes glinting cruelly. "I've *screamed* it."

Her words hit me like a slap, a crude and biting reminder of her intimate relationship with my father. My cheeks burn with anger and humiliation, a turmoil of emotions that leaves me momentarily speechless.

"Take her to her dressing room," she orders, her tone dismissive. "The ceremony will begin soon."

Rory's grip tightens as he leads me away, his expression impassive. The reality of my situation sets in with each step I take. I'm about to be forced into a marriage I never wanted, a token in Sharon's game for power and control.

I'm locked in a small, tastefully decorated dressing room, a surge of claustrophobia mixed with despair overcoming me. The walls—adorned with elegant wallpaper and soft lighting—seem to close in on me, a gilded cage mocking my predicament. I sink into an ornate chair, my mind racing as I grapple with the reality of my situation.

I could've tried to run, vanishing into the night, leaving this life of crime and manipulation behind. But the harsh truth is inescapable; without Sharon's resources, without the Flanagan name and its accompanying wealth, I am nothing in this city. Sharon controls everything—the finances, the connections, the power. On my own, I'd be a lamb amongst wolves, vulnerable and exposed in the merciless streets of Chicago.

My hands tremble as I think of the unknown man I'm about to marry, a man no doubt steeped in violence and danger, a man I've never even met. The thought of being bound to him, of being at the mercy of his whims and desires, fills me with a deep, unsettling fear.

I have to find a way out of this somehow. I can't let this be the end of my freedom.

I barely have a moment to myself before the door swings open again. Standing there—framed in the doorway—is Sharon, her expression a combination of smug satisfaction and cold practicality. My heart pounds with both fear and fury, the unfairness of my situation boiling over.

"What is going on? Who is he? And why am I being forced to marry a stranger without any prior notice?" I demand, my voice trembling with anger.

Sharon steps into the room, closing the door behind her with a soft click. "I suppose you deserve to know at least that much," she concedes with a shrug. "Your soon-to-be husband is Lukyan Ivanov."

The name hits me like a wave of icy water. Lukyan Ivanov, the eldest of the Ivanov brothers, a name whispered in hushed tones of fear and respect in the underworld of Chicago. Just hearing it sends chills up my spine.

"As for *why*, it's Carter," Sharon continues, referring to my stepbrother. "Your stepbrother has found himself in quite a bit of trouble with the Bratva, better known as the Russian mob. He owes them a significant sum."

"What the hell does that have to do with me?" I nearly spit.

"Offering a bride is the only way to settle his debt without bloodshed. Lukyan Ivanov agreed to the terms. On top of it all, this marriage will put a potential alliance with the

Bratva in play. It's an advantageous match for everyone involved."

Everyone involved but me. I feel like a sacrificial lamb, offered up to appease the monsters at our door. The very idea of being handed over to a man as dangerous as Lukyan Ivanov, all to clean up Carter's mess, is both terrifying and enraging.

"And what if I refuse?" I ask, even though I know the answer.

Sharon's smile is thin and cold. "You don't have that luxury. This marriage is happening with or without your consent. It's for the good of the family."

Her words sealed my fate, leaving me feeling helpless and trapped. I have no choice, no voice in this decision that will alter the course of my life forever.

"You have ten minutes before the ceremony begins. Freshen up as best you can. And don't get any ideas about leaving; there's no way out of this room. Besides, Rory's waiting just outside to make sure you don't scamper off."

"You won't get away with this," I snarl at her.

"My dear, I already have."

With that, she's gone.

Alone once more, I step in front of the full-length mirror that dominates one side of the dressing room, gazing at the reflection staring back at me. For a fleeting moment, the urge to rebel surges through me, to mess up my carefully styled hair, to smear the makeup that adorns my face. But then I think of Carter.

Despite his foolishness and the trouble he's caused, I can't shake the knowledge that his life no doubt truly hangs in the balance. He may be an idiot, and I may be furious with him, but I can't bear the thought of his life being snuffed out because of this mess. My hand falls away from my hair, the moment of rebellion passing.

Before I can dwell any longer, the door opens, and Rory stands there, his imposing figure filling the doorway. "It's time," he says, his deep voice devoid of emotion.

I nod silently, feeling as if I'm in a dream as he leads me back to the party. The crowd has shifted, now arranged in a manner reminiscent of a wedding ceremony, with an altar at the front and an officiant waiting. My heart races as I'm escorted toward the altar, each step feeling heavier than the last.

Then, I catch my first glimpse of my husband-to-be. He stands there like a statue carved from stone, his presence commanding the attention of everyone in the room. He's tall, his posture radiating confidence and power. His black hair is neatly styled, and his piercing blue eyes scan the crowd with a sharp intensity.

His strong jawline is set, and the tailored cut of his suit accentuates his broad shoulders. Despite the situation, I can't deny that he is incredibly handsome—in a dark and dangerous way.

But as I'm led closer, the reality of what's happening hits me once again.

I'm about to marry this man.

As I stand before Lukyan, his towering figure casts a shadow over me, his stony expression unyielding and intimidating. Despite the situation, his mere presence elicits a reaction within me that is both unsettling and undeniable. I feel a strange weakness, a stirring warmth that spreads through me, tingling between my thighs, leaving me bewildered.

No man has ever evoked such a response in me before. Why now, in this moment, of all moments?

My eyes are drawn to the scar that mars his face, a deep, jagged line running from his left temple to the corner of his jaw. It should be off-putting, a mark of violence and brutality. Yet, on Lukyan, it seems to add to his allure, giving him an air of rugged, unchained charisma.

The officiant begins the ceremony, his words a blur as I struggle to grasp the reality that I am marrying this stranger. Lukyan's voice is deep and resonant when he speaks his vows, the words "I do" cutting through the haze of my thoughts.

Then comes the kiss. It's perfunctory—a mere formality in this bizarre ritual—but the moment his lips touch mine, a shockwave of sensation ripples through me. The contact is brief, but it leaves me feeling unsteady as if I might melt right there at the altar.

He slips a ring on my finger, and just like that, it's over. I am now married to Lukyan Ivanov.

CHAPTER 2

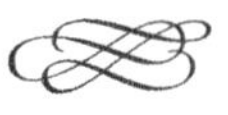

MAURA

The sounds of celebration fill the air as the wedding party carries on, a blend of Russian and Irish mob figures mingling in the grand ballroom. Glasses clink, and laughter echoes around me as I'm engulfed in a sea of well-wishes.

"Mrs. Ivanova, congratulations!" a burly man with a thick Russian accent exclaims, shaking my hand enthusiastically. " I never thought I'd see the day when the Flanagans and Ivanovs joined forces."

I force a smile, nodding politely while my mind races with anger and frustration. "Thank you," I manage to say, my voice steady despite the turmoil inside.

A stern-looking man with a Russian accent steps forward. "You must be very happy, da? Lukyan is a good man, strong man."

"Yes, very happy," I reply, my words feeling hollow.

As I navigate through the crowd, a woman adorned in expensive jewelry stops me before leaning in with a curious expression. "Darling, why aren't you spending time with your new husband? It's not every day a woman marries into the Bratva."

Caught off guard by her question, I quickly fabricate a response. "Oh, my feet are just killing me from these heels, and honestly, I'm so giddy about everything that I can barely keep my head on straight," I say with a laugh that I hope sounds genuine.

She nods, seemingly satisfied with my answer. "Well, make sure you enjoy your night. It's a big moment for both families."

I thank her and move away, feeling like an actor in a play I never auditioned for. Each congratulations and smile feels like a mask over the reality of my situation. I am now Maura Ivanova, wife to a Bratva king. A wife who was blindsided into marrying her husband is still struggling to wrap her head around what just happened.

Despite the whirlwind of emotions churning inside me, I find my attention repeatedly drawn to Luk, as I've heard others call him. He moves through the crowd with an effortless grace, exuding a sense of power and control that seems to set him apart from everyone else. There's something about his presence, a kind of fearless aura that captivates and intimidates in equal measure.

My eyes drift to his hands, strong and commanding. There's a certain finality in their movements, and I have no doubt that they have been instruments of violence, tools in the brutal world he inhabits. It's a chilling thought, yet I can't seem to look away.

Near him, a small group of men and one woman who shares his imposing stature and sharp features catch my attention. Their resemblance to Luk is unmistakable—they must be his siblings.

Suddenly, Luk's gaze shifts in my direction, and our eyes meet for a fleeting moment. The intensity in his blue eyes is jarring, and I quickly avert my gaze, my cheeks warming slightly. I chastise myself internally; he's got me acting like a nervous teenager, flustered by a mere glance.

Before I can gather my thoughts, Sharon appears at my side, her expression one of thinly veiled irritation. "You're being a wallflower at your own damn wedding," she scolds, her voice low but sharp. "This is your night. Act like it."

I can't help but scoff, the absurdity of the situation suddenly striking me. "My night?" I laugh bitterly. "You make it sound like this is the wedding I've dreamed about all my life, not something I was forced into without a moment's notice."

Sharon's eyes narrow dangerously at my response, her voice icy. "In case you haven't figured it out yet, my dear, what you want is the lowest priority here. This is about more than just you."

I open my mouth, a sharp retort on the tip of my tongue, ready to challenge her callous disregard for my life. But before I can utter a single word, the atmosphere shifts dramatically.

A man breaks through the crowd; his movements are swift, his eyes burning with a fierce intensity. The room seems to freeze as he approaches, his focus locked on me. Sharon tries to question him, "Who the hell are you?" but he doesn't even acknowledge her. In one fluid motion, he draws a gun, his intention clear as he aims directly at me. The realization of what's about to happen hits me like a tidal wave, fear and disbelief coursing through me as the man prepares to fire.

My breath catches in my throat as I stare at the gun, its barrel a dark, ominous tunnel pointing straight at me. Time seems to slow down, and my heart is pounding in my ears. But before the man can pull the trigger, a blur of motion catches the corner of my eye.

A huge, imposing figure lunges forward, his movements a blend of speed and deadly precision. He grabs the assailant's wrist, twisting it with a force that produces a sickening crack. The gun slips from the attacker's grasp, but the man catches it effortlessly before it hits the floor, tucking it securely into the back of his waistband.

Only then do I dare to look up at him.

Luk, my husband, stands towering over the would-be assassin. His face is a mask of controlled fury, his blue eyes cold and hard. Without a word, he delivers a punishing strike to the man's face, sending him sprawling to the floor. Gasps sound from the crowd.

The attacker, dazed but not defeated, scrambles for a second weapon hidden at his ankle. But Luk is relentless, his rage obvious. He unleashes a barrage of blows, each one landing with a brutality that leaves the partygoers frozen in shock and horror.

Luk's fury is like a force of nature, unstoppable and fierce. The man beneath him stands no chance; each attempt to defend himself is met with an even more vicious response. Luk beats him to the edge of consciousness, the severity of the attack leaving the assailant barely clinging to life.

The room is silent, the previous merriment replaced by an invasive sense of dread and fear.

As I stand there, frozen in shock, two men quickly approach Luk, their expressions grim but controlled. They're the same men I noticed earlier, the ones who bear a striking resemblance to my husband.

"Enough, brother!" one of them commands, his voice firm as he and the other man pull Luk away from the brutalized assailant. "He's more useful to us alive than dead. We can get information out of him."

Luk, still seething with barely contained rage, pauses and then nods tersely in agreement.

They lift the unconscious man with ease, carrying him out of the room as the crowd parts to let them through. Luk watches, his chest rising and falling with deep, slow breaths, his expression stony. The tension in the air is tangible, the violence having shattered the festive atmosphere.

Meanwhile, Sharon steps forward, trying to regain control over the situation that is quickly spiraling out of control. "Let the band play," she orders sharply. "Everyone, please continue with the celebration."

As the music starts up again, an awkward attempt to restore normalcy, my heart pounds against my ribcage, my eyes lingering on the small pools of blood on the floor that belong to the would-be assassin.

The world my father had always shielded me from now stares me in the face, raw and unfiltered. My mind races with the implications of what this means for my future, my safety, and the true nature of the man I've just married.

As the guests attempt to recapture the gala mood of the party as if nothing happened, my gaze remains locked on Luk. His hands are stained with blood, a startling contrast to his pale skin, and there's a smear of red on his face. The fight has disrupted his perfect composure; his hair, once slicked back meticulously, is now disheveled, with a few thick strands falling across his forehead, giving him the look of a wild man.

Luk pulls a handkerchief from his inner coat pocket and wipes the blood from his hands and face with an apathetic efficiency that speaks of his familiarity with such situations.

I know I shouldn't feel this way, but there's something undeniably compelling about Luk at that moment. He looks like a predator, a creature that has just defended its territory. The raw power and primal energy he exudes are strangely alluring, stirring something within me that I can't quite put my finger on.

More than that, the realization that he would have killed the man who threatened causes gooseflesh to erupt on my arms. Even if Luk sees me as nothing more than his property, his willingness to protect me at all costs is impressive. My heart races as our eyes meet; the intensity of his gaze captivates me.

Luk strides toward me, his expression unreadable but for a glint in his eyes that resembles hunger. I start to awkwardly stammer out a thank you, unsure of how else to respond to the violence he just unleashed to protect me. But he cuts me off, making it clear that gratitude is not what he's after.

"Come."

His grip on my arm is firm but not painful, and despite the situation, I feel a thrill shoot through me at his touch. He leads me away from the ballroom, away from the eyes of the mobsters and their hushed whispers.

As we leave, I catch a glimpse of Sharon watching us with a satisfied smirk. Her expression sends a wave of disgust through me, but I also feel a hint of relief at getting away from her.

"Where are we going?" I ask quietly as we navigate the hotel's corridors.

Luk doesn't look at me as he answers, his voice low and controlled. "It's time for us to consummate our marriage."

His words send a wave of fear, curiosity, and inexplicable excitement through me. I'm about to be alone with this man, a man who is now my husband yet remains a stranger to me. A man capable of brutal violence, yet who just saved my life.

The irony of my situation is not lost on me. I'm leaving behind one kind of monster only to jump into bed with another.

CHAPTER 3

MAURA

Luk leads me through the opulent hallways of the hotel, our footsteps echoing softly on the marble floor. We approach an elevator and ascend to the top floor, where he unlocks the door to a penthouse suite that exudes old-world luxury, seamlessly blended with modern touches.

The suite is spacious, with high ceilings and grand windows that offer a breathtaking view of Chicago's skyline. The furniture is a blend of rich, dark woods and plush fabrics, and contemporary art pieces dot the walls, adding a touch of modern sophistication to the classic surroundings.

My heart pounds in my chest as I take in the setting.

"Is this your usual suite?" I ask, my voice tinged with nervous interest.

"Yes," Luk replies curtly, briefly glancing around the room before his eyes settle back on me.

"Are the men you were with tonight your family?" I ask, hoping to learn more about his life. And that woman is your sister?"

"Correct," he answers, his tone giving nothing else away.

Luk moves to a small bar area, his movements precise as he prepares two drinks. The clink of ice into a glass and the splash of liquid are the only sounds in the otherwise uncomfortable silence that fills the room.

He offers me one of the glasses, but I hesitate. "No, thank you." Although a drink sounds like heaven, especially under the circumstances, I want to keep my wits about me.

Luk doesn't insist. He simply takes a sip from his own glass, his gaze sweeping over me. Those blue eyes—hungry and sensual—seem to see right through me. I stand there, caught in his intense stare, feeling a confusing combination of fear and attraction.

He steps over to the expansive window, his silhouette framed against the glittering backdrop of the skyline. The city lights twinkle like distant stars, casting a soft glow on his features. He takes a slow sip of his drink as he gazes at the view outside.

"You are my wife," he says, the hint of a Russian accent coloring his words. His statement hangs in the air, a simple fact laden with complex implications.

"Yes," I reply, my voice barely above a whisper. His tone is unreadable, leaving me unsure whether he's stating a fact or expressing an emotion. "I suppose I am."

He turns to face me, his eyes piercing as he takes another sip. "Remove your dress," he commands, his voice low but firm.

My first instinct is to rebel, to assert my autonomy, and to refuse his order.

No way. The words form in my mind, but they don't make it past my lips.

He holds my gaze, unflinching, then says, "We are married, and this is our wedding night." Then, in a slightly softer tone, he adds, "And I have wanted you like mad since the moment I laid eyes on you."

His admission catches me off guard and sends my heart racing. There's an intensity in his eyes that's both intimidating and alluring. Compelled by his words and an unexpected desire, I find my hands moving of their own accord.

With trembling fingers, I reach for the zipper at the back of my dress. The fabric slowly slips away, revealing my skin inch by inch, the dress cascading to the floor in a whisper of silk. I stand there, vulnerable and exposed, under my new husband's intense stare.

As I stand there in my underwear, feeling exposed yet strangely empowered, Luk approaches me. His eyes trace over every curve and contour of my body. I'm surprised to find myself reveling in his inspection, the way he looks at me stirring something deep within. My pussy clenches, yearning for him.

My emotions are all over the place—desire mingled with resentment; attraction coupled with apprehension. It's all so overwhelming, so intense, and happening far too quickly.

When he's close enough to touch, his attention shifts to the bruises marring my skin. He gently lifts my arm, examining the marks with a scrutiny that sends a shiver down my spine. His expression darkens, a fierce protectiveness flashing in his eyes. It's clear he would like to punish the one responsible for these injuries.

I quickly fabricate a lie. "These bruises are from the family's Great Danes. They love to roughhouse," I say, trying to sound casual.

The truth, however, is far more sinister. Rory, Sharon's loyal goon, is responsible for the bruises, but it was she who gave the orders. However, I can't bring myself to reveal this to Luk as yet.

Luk's gaze lingers on the discolorations a moment longer before meeting my eyes. There's a depth in his look that suggests he sees through my lie, an understanding that there's more to the story than I'm willing to share. But he doesn't press the issue and doesn't question me further.

Without another word, he wraps his strong arm around my waist, pulling me close. The suddenness of his movement takes me by surprise, but before I can react, his lips are on mine, and he's kissing me deeply. The firmness of his body against mine and the taste of whiskey on his tongue brings with it a rush of desire unlike anything I've ever experienced. I can feel his hardness through his dark slacks. The sensation of his stiff cock pressing against me makes my heart race even faster.

My movements feel like a puppet master is orchestrating them as my hands reach up to his shirt, fingers working to undo the buttons. I push his shirt off his shoulders, revealing a lean upper body marked by a landscape of scars and Bratva tattoos that speak of violence and family loyalty.

Luk remains in total command of the situation; his movements are sure and assertive. To my surprise, I find myself relishing this dynamic and the way he takes charge. His strength is reassuring, his dominance an unexpected source of comfort.

With effortless ease, he scoops me up in his arms and carries me to the bed. The world around us fades away, leaving only the two of us in this intimate, charged space.

Once I'm on the bed, he steps back and looks down at me. Something about the way he regards me with those gorgeous, ice-blue eyes nearly undoes me.

"You're beautiful."

His words cause me to shiver all over, yet I also feel a surge of warmth.

"So are you."

My own words sound woefully insufficient. With his shirt open and his sculpted, powerful torso on full display, Luk is unbelievably attractive. But he doesn't move, it's as if he wants me to understand that we're on *his* time, that nothing happens until he wills it.

Finally, after several long, teasing moments, he lunges forward with the grace and power of a jungle cat. He leans down, covering me with kisses as he moves down my body. His hands reach behind me, and I arch in response. He quickly undoes the clasp of my bra and slips it off, then buries his face in between my breasts, licking and suckling them.

"Oh, oh my God."

The words pour out of me as Luk takes the nipple of my right breast in his mouth, tonguing it with expert skill. He soon moves to the other, causing both nipples to harden. My panties are soaked with arousal. He flicks those stunning blue eyes up at me as he moves down further, kissing the gentle curve of my belly. He pulls my panties off before moving over the small patch of red hair above my pussy, then spreads my thighs.

Just like that, I'm completely nude in front of a man I only met an hour ago. But it's strange. The situation, odd as it is, feels right.

What's going on?

Without a word, he begins to eat me out. I moan at the first sensation of his tongue against my lips. Luk knows exactly how to tease me, how to move his tongue tantalizingly close to my clit but deny me precisely what I want.

I open my mouth and let out a soft moan as he finally gives my clit the attention I've been craving. He makes slow circles with his tongue, each movement sending a fresh wave of pleasure through my body. It isn't easy, but I manage to open my eyes to take in the sight of him at work.

His big, strong hands are on my thighs, holding them open. I can see his toned body, his blue eyes glancing up at me here and there as he licks. After a time, his hands slide up my body, taking hold of my breasts again, his fingers teasing my nipples.

"Luk... that feels..."

It's too much to take. Between the sensation of his lips and tongue on my clit, and his hands on my breasts, an orgasm is inevitable. I cross the border, my back arching again as I let out a scream of total delight. The ecstasy is incredible; Luk is making me feel like I never have before.

When the orgasm fades, I fall flat on my back. Luk stands up, wiping my juices from his mouth with the back of his hand. He regards me with intensity as if surveying the quality of his work by how I look in the aftermath.

"Please," I say finally. "Take off your clothes."

He smirks slightly, as if he knows he's got me right where he wants me. But he does as I ask, slipping off his shirt and tossing it aside before undoing his belt and zipper. Soon he's in nothing but a pair of tight, black boxer briefs that cling to his powerful thick thighs and the muscular curve of his ass.

Not to mention the massive erection he's sporting.

He pulls his underwear down, his cock, thick and hard, springing out. It's big, bigger than I'd imagined. Once he's bare, he moves on top of me, causing a thrill to run through my body as his manhood drags against my inner thigh.

"Wait."

He freezes when I say the word, giving me the impression that he will not do anything I'm uncomfortable with.

"What is it?"

He's warm and solid against me, and it's hard not to simply give in and tell him to take me. But there's something that needs to be said.

"It's... I've... I've never done this before." My cheeks turn hot.

His eyes flash. "I know."

He knows? It seems odd at first. But then I remember how Sharon always guarded me from men, how she'd always been insistent that I stay a virgin. It dawns on me that this hadn't simply been about control but as a way to make me more enticing as a bargaining chip.

"We can wait," he says. "But make no mistake, I'm going to make you mine."

Another shudder of fear and arousal. What is this effect Luk has on me?

Part of me wants to take him up on the offer to postpone it, but the greater part wants him to claim me.

I make a decision.

I wrap my legs around his hips, guiding him closer. He allows the slightest hint of a smile before positioning himself right on top of me, his cock dragging against my soaking-wet lips. I want him, I need him, and I still don't understand how he's making me feel this way.

His head is at my entrance. I look down, realizing that a mere push of his hips is all that separates me from no longer being a virgin.

"Please." The word slips from my lips.

He gives me what I want.

Luk pushes slowly and gently, his head sinking into me, followed by the next few inches of his manhood.

The sensation is like nothing I've ever felt. There's pleasure, there's pain, and then there's that way he looks at me with those blue eyes.

I moan, squirming underneath him as he takes my virginity with one deep thrust. I feel as if I'm being split in half in the best way possible, pleasure and pain flowing outward from where he enters me. Even though the heart of an animal needing to rut beats inside of him, Luk is tender and patient, knowing that he has to use care.

Eventually, he bottoms out. His cock is huge, so big that I'd been certain he wouldn't be able to fit inside me. Yet when I open my eyes, he's sunken all the way between my legs. Slowly, he pulls back, his dick glistening with my juices. Then he pushes in again. This time, he enters me with more ease, my walls stretching to accommodate him. The following thrusts are even easier. Soon, it feels as if he's made for me, his cock fitting like a key into its lock.

As I watch him on top of me, his powerful body at work, muscles moving underneath tattooed flesh, I find myself growing bolder. Something about Luk makes me feel comfortable giving myself over in a way I never thought I would. I wrap my legs tightly around him, clamp my hands down onto that perfect ass, and moan hard into his ear.

It's not long before I feel another orgasm on the brink.

"Come with me," I beg. "Please."

I'd said my piece, but there's no doubt that Luk would come when he was good and ready.

Sure enough, he opens his eyes and looks down at me.

"You first."

There's no resisting it. I come hard, this time feeling like I'm about to unravel beneath him. Every bit of my body lights up with white-hot fire, pleasure assailing me from all angles. Right when I reach my peak, Luk comes too. His manhood erupts, pulsing with his orgasm. He grunts hard, his muscles clenching as he spills inside me, filling me with his hot seed.

I hold him close, wanting every drop of him inside me. He's more than happy to oblige.

When our climaxes fade, he falls to my side and wraps me up in his arms, a surprising amount of warmth between us.

A whirlwind of emotions envelop me. I'm feeling exhilarated from the closeness we've just shared, yet simultaneously uneasy. Feelings of guilt and pleasure intertwine in a confusing dance, leaving me unsure of where one ends and the other begins.

Despite the turmoil within me, I can't deny the sense of security that Luk's presence provides. His warmth, his strength, it's all so reassuring, so different from what I expected.

"You are my wife," he says again, his chest rumbling with his deep, powerful voice. It's as if he keeps saying the words; it will become more real.

"I am."

It's a strange feeling to be this close to someone who was a stranger only hours ago yet now feels so integral to my existence.

CHAPTER 4

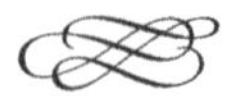

LUK

"We need to discuss the expansion plans," I begin, my voice low and firm. "Both for Ivanov Holdings and our Bratva operations."

My brother Lev leans forward, his eyes narrowing slightly. "The West Side is ripe for the taking. We've already got a foothold there; we just need to push a bit harder."

I nod, considering his words. "Agreed, but we need to be strategic about it. Brute force won't win this. It's a chess game, not a street fight."

It's late morning the next day, and I'm sitting in my study at home, a room that breathes the essence of old-school sophistication. The walls are lined with dark wood paneling, and the heavy leather furniture speaks of a time when craftsmanship was revered. The air is thick with the scent of aged books and the subtle hint of cigar smoke, a remnant of countless late-night discussions.

My brothers, Yuri and Lev, are seated across from me. Yuri's lean frame is relaxed, but his eyes, sharp as ever, miss nothing. Lev, always more intense, sits with a rigid posture, his black hair and grey-blue eyes giving him a look that's as distinguished as it is unpredictable. His military background and expertise in interrogation make him an invaluable asset to the Bratva, but his unpredictability is a constant concern.

Yuri chimes in, his tone measured. "Financially, we're positioned well for an expansion, but we need to cover our tracks. Laundering the money through the new construction projects is the best way to go."

His way with numbers has always been his strength, and his ability to navigate the complex financial waters of our business is unmatched. "Good," I say. "Ensure that everything looks clean. The last thing we need is unwanted attention."

Lev's gaze shifts to me, a flicker of something like ambition in his eyes. "What about the O'Malleys' territories? There's a weakness there we can exploit."

I lean back in my chair, considering his proposal. "It's a risky move, but it could pay off. We'll need to be careful, however. The O'Malleys aren't going to roll over without a fight."

As our business discussion progresses, I find my thoughts drifting as images of Maura invade my mind unbidden. Last night's memory is vivid—the feeling of her fair skin, her long, lustrous red hair, and the expression on her face when she reached her peak. It's disconcerting how pervasive these thoughts are.

"Hey, Luk," Lev's voice cuts through my reverie, a teasing edge in his tone. "You with us, or still in the bedroom?"

I shoot him a sharp look, irritation flaring momentarily. "Focus, Lev," I retort, trying to steer my mind back to the matters at hand.

He laughs. "I could say the same to you, brother."

Just then, our sister, Elena, walks into the room, her presence a blend of confidence and understated elegance. She catches the tail end of the conversation and, with her usual perceptiveness, picks up on the underlying subject.

"There's more to Maura than just her beauty, Luk," she advises as she sits down in one of the office's high-backed leather wing chairs, her tone serious despite the teasing glint in her eyes. She's obviously smart and has inside knowledge of the Irish mafia. She could be a valuable asset."

I've never been one to discuss my personal life openly, especially not in terms of romantic relationships. "We have more important things to focus on," I say, attempting to redirect the conversation back to business.

Lev smirks at my sharp response, clearly enjoying the rare opportunity to tease me. "Come on, brother, you can't blame me for noticing. It's not every day Luk Ivanov gets distracted, especially by a woman."

Elena's gaze flicks between us. "Maura's not just any woman, Lev. She's clearly clever and accommodating. She played her part well last night. I think there's more to her than meets the eye." She grins. "Even though there's no doubt that her looks heavily factored into your decision to agree to the marriage."

I want to dispute her, but she speaks the truth. I'd been engaged to somebody else, but when the offer for Maura—

none other than Sharon Halsey's beautiful, virgin step-daughter—was presented to me, there was no resisting.

I feel a twinge of annoyance at the conversation's turn. "Elena, Lev, let's keep our focus on the business. We have expansion plans to finalize, and let's leave my choice of wife out of it," I say, trying to steer the conversation back to less personal matters.

But Elena isn't so easily deterred. "I'm just saying that a woman like Maura could become a significant player in our world. Don't underestimate her, Luk."

Her words linger in the air, a reminder that Maura's role in my life—and potentially in the broader scope of our family's operations—might be more complicated than I initially thought.

Lev leans back in his chair, his expression amused. "All right, all right, back to business. But you have to admit, marriage suits you. I can already tell."

Before I can respond, there's a knock on the door. "Come in," I call out, grateful for the interruption.

Grigori Petrov, my arms dealer and close friend, steps into the study. With his dark brown hair, bold brown eyes, and sharp jawline that hints at his Slavic heritage, his presence is commanding. His face bears the scars that tell tales of past missions as an arms dealer and enforcer. He's a man who embodies the rougher side of our world. His gaze briefly meets Elena's, a look passing between them that I notice but choose not to comment on.

"What's going on, Grigori?" I ask, my impatient tone indicating that I expect straight answers.

Grigori's expression is grim. "The would-be assassin from last night—he's dead. He didn't last long under questioning."

"Maybe you should've been gentler on him, brother," Elena says, a hint of criticism in her voice. If the fool were still alive, we could have gotten more information out of him."

Grigori nods his head, confirming, "He barely said a word before he died. There wasn't much time to get anything useful."

I feel a surge of rage within me. I regret the loss of a potential source of intel, but I don't regret killing the man who tried to take Maura's life. If anything, he got off easy. The instinct to protect her, to eliminate any threat to her, overrode any rational thought of gathering intelligence.

"The man tried to kill my wife," I say, my voice hard as steel. "I won't apologize for dealing with a threat to my family. We'll find other ways to get the information we need."

The room falls into a tense silence, the weight of my words hanging heavily in the air. My brothers and Grigori understand the unspoken code—family comes first, always.

"It could be a power play from a rival family," Lev suggests, leaning forward with a frown. "The O'Malleys or the Morettis, maybe. They've always been looking for a way to weaken us."

Yuri, tapping his fingers thoughtfully on the table, adds his perspective. "Or it could be something internal, a betrayal from within. We can't rule out the possibility of someone trying to move up in the ranks."

Elena, her expression thoughtful, chimes in with a different angle. “Don't forget what’s happened in the past. There could be someone holding a grudge, waiting for the right moment to strike back at us.”

Throughout the discussion, Grigori remains mostly silent, his eyes moving from one speaker to the next, assessing each theory with a critical eye.

The more we talk, the clearer it becomes that the assassination attempt wasn't just a random act of violence. The attack was calculated, a deliberate move to strike at the heart of the Ivanov family. It wasn't just about me; it was an attempt to destabilize our operations, to send a message.

As the theories continue to swirl, I find myself deep in thought, piecing together the fragments of information and intuition. The realization that someone out there not only wanted to hurt me but also wanted to see me suffer is a chilling thought.

The room buzzes with speculation when I suddenly raise my hand, signaling for silence. "I might have an idea who was behind this," I say, the pieces of the puzzle starting to form a clearer picture in my mind.

The room falls quiet, and all eyes are on me. I know that what I'm about to suggest could change the course of our next moves and, potentially, the fate of our family.

CHAPTER 5

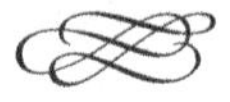

MAURA

"Holy shit."

The words, inelegant though they may be, tumble out of my mouth as I take in the sight of my new home.

It's late in the morning when I find myself standing before Luk's house, the sunlight casting a warm glow over its impressive façade. The mansion, nestled in the heart of Chicago's Gold Coast, exudes old-world charm and grandeur. It's a stunning piece of architecture, with intricate stone carvings adorning its exterior and large, arched windows that offer glimpses of the opulence within.

The building stands tall and imposing, a testament to its owner's power and wealth. Ivy creeps up its sides, softening the stone's stern lines, while manicured gardens add a touch of color and life to the stately home.

As I approach the door, my mind flashes back to earlier this morning. I had woken up in the plush, king-sized bed of our downtown hotel room, feeling a chill from the empty space beside me where I had expected to find Luk. Instead, he was gone.

On the pillow, I found a note written in his neat, precise handwriting. It explained that he had to attend to family business matters but urged me to take my time and call the driver when I was ready to come home. The word *home* echoes in my mind, a concept that feels both foreign and daunting.

I stand before the grand entrance, unable to shake the surreal feeling that envelops me. This new life as Luk's wife stretches out before me, filled with uncertainties and new responsibilities.

Last night was a blend of passion and a connection that I had never experienced before. Yet, despite the intensity of our encounter, I can't help but feel unprepared for the role I'm about to step into. Being a wife—especially in Luk's world—comes with its own set of rules and expectations, ones that I'm not yet sure I understand or am ready to fulfill. Though I grew up around the Irish mob, I was largely shielded from its darker parts.

Taking a deep breath, I push the door open and step inside.

The entry hall unfolds before me in a display of grandeur and elegance. It reminds me of an English country manor, with its high, ornate ceilings and a sweeping staircase that curves gracefully toward the upper floors. The floor is a polished marble, reflecting the soft light filtering in through tall, arched windows. Rich tapestries and portraits adorn the walls, each telling a story of heritage and legacy.

Staff moves quietly and efficiently through the hall, their presence a subtle reminder of the life I've stepped into. The wealth I grew up in was clearly not as great as Luk's. The staff pauses as they notice me, offering greetings with a respectful deference.

"Good morning, Mrs. Ivanova," a middle-aged butler says, his posture rigid. "We hope you find everything to your liking."

"Thank you," I reply, still adjusting to being addressed with such formality and with my new surname.

"Is there anything you require, ma'am?" asks a young maid with a friendly smile.

"Just finding my way around for now, thank you," I say, trying to sound more confident than I feel.

As I move through the hall, I realize that I'm quite hungry. My stomach reminds me that I'd skipped breakfast in the rush of the morning. Guided by the smell of fresh coffee and baked bread, I make my way to the kitchen.

The kitchen is a warm, inviting space, contrasting with the formality of the rest of the house. It's large and well-equipped, with a homey feel that immediately puts me at ease. The smell of food and the sound of sizzling from the stove creates a comforting ambiance, a reminder of the simple pleasures of home.

There's a bustling team of cooks, each busy with their tasks. I notice that the kitchen is stocked with everything I could possibly need.

I step into the large, walk-in pantry and begin to reach for some ingredients. Immediately, one of the cooks, a pretty young woman with a bright, engaging smile, steps forward. She looks to be a few years younger than me, with curly auburn hair tied back in a neat bun and sparkling green eyes that radiate warmth and friendliness.

"Oh, please allow me, Mrs. Ivanova," she says, her tone both gentle and insistent. "I'll prepare something for you."

Accustomed to doing things for myself, I hesitate. "It's really okay, I can make something," I say, not wanting to impose.

Her amusement at my response is evident. "I insist, Mrs. Ivanova. It's my job, after all. And besides," she adds with a playful glint in her eye, "Mr. Ivanov would be quite incensed at the idea of his new wife having to make her own food on her first day here."

Her words bring a smile to my face, and I find myself relenting. "All right if you insist. Thank you."

As she busies herself with preparing something for me, we make our introductions. "I'm Maura, by the way. But I guess you already know that."

"I'm Lily," she replies with a friendly nod. "Welcome to the Ivanov home, your home. If you need anything, just let me know."

As Lily skillfully prepares a simple yet appetizing salad, our conversation flows easily. I watch as she deftly slices and dices the vegetables, admiring her evident skills in the kitchen.

"I've never really been one to be waited on," I share, watching her work. "This is all quite new to me."

Lily looks up, a hint of surprise in her eyes. "Really? I heard you were like royalty in your own family."

I chuckle lightly, shaking my head. "It wasn't quite like that," I tell her. The truth is more complicated; Sharon's version of a gilded cage was one where I was left to fend for myself within the confines of our home. But I keep these details to myself, not wanting to delve too deeply into my past with someone I just met.

Lily's expression shifts to one of mild embarrassment. "I'm sorry. I didn't mean to be so familiar."

I offer her a reassuring smile. "There's nothing to apologize for. It's nice to have a casual conversation."

She nods, a relieved smile on her face, and then presents the salad to me. "Here you go. I hope you like it."

"It looks wonderful; thank you, Lily," I say, genuinely grateful for her kindness and company.

While eating, I continue chatting with Lily. "I've only been here for a short while, but everyone's been so nice," I tell her, genuinely surprised by the hospitality I've encountered since I arrived. "It's very different from what I expected."

Lily laughs, a warm, infectious sound. "The Ivanovs definitely run a tight ship, but they're far from tyrants. They treat their staff well, and in return, we're all fiercely loyal to them. It's more like a big, somewhat unconventional family."

Her words are reassuring, painting a picture of a household that's in stark contrast to the harsh, unforgiving world I've always associated with the Bratva. "That's really good to hear," I reply, feeling a bit more at ease. "I guess I had a certain image in my mind of what life here would be like."

Lily nods understandingly. "It's natural to have preconceptions, especially with all the stories out there about the Ivanovs. But you'll find that there's more to this place than meets the eye."

She checks her watch, her eyes flashing.

"Shoot. I should get going. I have lots of food prep for tonight. It was nice meeting you, Mrs. Ivanova. Welcome home," Lily says, her tone warm and welcoming. And please, let me know if there's anything else I can do for you."

"I will. And thanks, Lily."

With a smile, she turns her attention back to her duties.

As I savor the salad, the side door to the kitchen opens, and a woman enters. She's young, with long, black hair that cascades down her back and eyes that are a striking shade of blue. Her features resemble Luk's, and I remember seeing her briefly at the wedding.

The woman looks over the kitchen with an inquisitive gaze before her eyes land on me. "Why are you eating in the kitchen like a cook on a break? Don't tell me you're too shy for the dining room?" she says. Like her brother, there's a faint hint of a Russian accent in her speech.

I can't help but smile at her frankness. "I just arrived and found myself here. It's quite comfortable, actually."

Elena snorts lightly, her amusement evident. "Well, perhaps I should introduce myself properly. I'm Elena Ivanova, Luk's sister."

"I'm Maura," I reply, extending my hand. As we shake hands, I can't help but take note of Elena's presence. Despite her almost otherworldly beauty, she carries herself with a strength and confidence that's immediately apparent. It's no doubt a side effect of growing up with three brothers in a world as complex and demanding as the Bratva.

Elena's curiosity seems piqued as she asks, "So, what do you think of the place so far?"

I pause for a moment, looking around the kitchen before answering. "It's impressive, definitely. And a little overwhelming, to be honest."

Elena laughs at my response, a sound that's both carefree and infectious. She reaches toward my salad, her fingers aiming for a cherry tomato. In a playful reflex, I quickly poke the tomato with my fork and pop it into my mouth just as Elena is about to grab it.

Her eyes widen in mock surprise before she bursts into laughter. "You're quick! I like that."

Elena's delight is clear, and I can't help but join in the laughter. There's an ease to her demeanor that makes the interaction feel light and comfortable.

Without missing a beat, Elena announces, "Well, you better hurry up with that salad. I've been appointed as your official tour guide so it would seem. There's a lot more to see."

Her offer surprises me, but the prospect of exploring the mansion with someone as down-to-earth as Elena is appealing. Finishing the last of my salad, I stand up, ready to follow her. "Lead the way, then," I say with a smile.

Elena guides me through the expansive three-story mansion, which is nothing short of a labyrinth of luxury. Every room she shows me is beautifully and tastefully decorated with plush furnishings. The walls are decorated with tasteful art, and floor-to-ceiling windows bathe everything in natural light. The formal dining room is grand, with a long table made of rich, dark wood that could easily seat twenty people. An ornate chandelier hangs overhead.

As we move through the house, I find myself increasingly drawn to Elena's confidence and brazenness. Her candidness is refreshing, and her familiarity with the mansion makes the tour not just informative but genuinely enjoyable.

"My brother sends his apologies for not being able to greet you himself," she says, our footsteps echoing through the vast halls. "It's just that with the business last night, the assassin... well, there's much work to be done."

The attempt on my life last night flashes through my mind —the gun pointed at me, the man's face twisted in anger, the way Luk intervened, protecting me with a savage ferocity that was unexpected. I had only survived the attack because of Luk.

"I understand."

She nods. "He'll get to the bottom of it; correction, *we'll* get to the bottom of it. No one makes a move on an Ivanov like that without paying a steep price."

"Have you learned anything so far?"

"Unfortunately, no. The assassin... let's just say he's not going to be telling his life story anytime soon."

I understand her implication. A chill runs through me at the knowledge that he's dead.

"Please know you're safe here," she quickly adds. "This place isn't just for show; it's built like a fortress."

"That's good to know."

Finally, Elena leads me to a room she calls "your personal bedroom." It's as beautifully decorated as the other rooms, with a large, comfortable-looking bed draped in fine linens at its center. The room features a cozy sitting area with a fireplace and some doors open to a balcony from which I can view the landscaped grounds.

"You and Luk will share the master bedroom, of course. But this is your own space should you need or want it."

"It's lovely."

Eventually, she announces, "Now, it's time to show you the best part." She leads me through a set of French doors on the first level, and we step into a stunning English garden. It's a picturesque oasis with raised flowerbeds and neatly trimmed hedges. Stone pathways meander through it, leading to various secluded niches with stone benches. A small fountain is the centerpiece of the garden, the gentle trickling of the water adding to the serene atmosphere.

As we walk through the garden, Elena points out various features with pride and affection. "That rose bush over there," she gestures, "is older than I am. It's always the first one to bloom."

Just then, one of the doors across the garden swings open, and three men step out. I recognize two of them from the wedding.

"Are those your brothers?" I ask, nodding in their direction.

Elena follows my gaze and nods. "Yes, that's Lev and Yuri. And the guy who looks like he's stepped out of a mafia movie poster? That's Grigori, Luk's right-hand man. He's an arms dealer, enforcer, and childhood friend. He's basically a jack-of-all-trades in our world."

There's a certain admiration in her voice as she talks about Grigori, her gaze lingering on him a moment longer than her brothers. I sense there's more she wants to say about Grigori, but I decide not to pry.

Elena continues. "Don't let their tough exteriors fool you. They're big softies at heart. Well, except when they have to be tough, which is...actually, quite often."

The way she casually navigates the complexities of her family's dynamics is both disarming and endearing. I can't help but chuckle at her description.

"They seem formidable, for sure," I comment, watching the brothers and Grigori confer with their heads together.

Elena shrugs, a playful smirk on her lips. "Formidable, charming, occasionally terrifying—that's the typical description of the men in the Ivanov Bratva. But to me, they're family. Around here, that's what really matters."

Elena turns back to me. "They probably came out here to talk about business matters. We can just ignore them."

Despite her nonchalant attitude, I can't help but feel wary around these men, who seem somewhat intimidating even at a distance.

I watch them for a moment longer. They interact with an ease and familiarity that speaks of a long and shared history. Yet, beneath the casual demeanor, I sense an undercurrent of something more sinister—undoubtedly related to the life they lead as members of a crime dynasty.

This garden may be a peaceful retreat, but I know that beyond its borders, there is a dangerous and frightening world.

CHAPTER 6

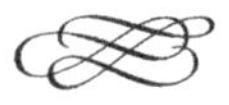

MAURA

"See these bushes? They're hydrangeas. They're one of my favorites in the entire garden," Elena says, gently touching the shrub, which is just beginning to bud. "The color of the blooms change depending on the pH of the soil. It's fascinating, really."

"I had no idea flowers could do that," I respond, genuinely intrigued.

Elena nods, her eyes bright with passion for the subject. "Oh, yes. The garden is full of little surprises like that. Come, see the hibiscus."

She leads me to another raised bed. "These will produce beautiful pink flowers that attract butterflies. The individual blooms don't last long, but when they flower, they're breathtaking."

I gaze at the plant, trying to picture it in bloom. "I'm sure they're stunning," I say softly.

Elena smiles, pleased. "I'm glad you like them. This garden is a bit of a sanctuary for me. I come here often to escape from daily pressures."

I listen intently as Elena continues to explain each plant we pass and describe its intricacies. Her enthusiasm for the garden is evident in her every word. But as much as I try to focus on what she's saying, my mind keeps drifting back to the events of last night.

Images involuntarily flood my mind. I picture Luk and his brothers—cold and merciless—extracting information from the man who tried to kill me. I imagine him being tortured and beaten to death. The thought of it is unsettling and a little overwhelming.

Suddenly, I freeze as dizziness envelops me. I feel like I might faint.

"Hey, are you okay?" Elena's voice sounds like it's coming from far away.

"It's... I..." I can't even form a coherent thought.

"Here. Come with me."

Elena quickly guides me to a nearby bench situated in front of the fountain. I listen to the sound of the water, but it doesn't calm me. I take a deep breath and try to steady my breathing.

Elena looks at me with concern. "Maura, what's wrong? You seem preoccupied."

I sigh and try to articulate what's on my mind. "It's everything. The wedding, the assassination attempt, this new life... it's all a little much to take in."

Elena nods with a look of understanding on her face. "I know it's a lot. Anyone would feel overwhelmed in a similar situation."

I shake my head, chastising myself. "I don't know why it's bothering me so much. I know what the world of Bratva is about. I'm not unaware of the violence it involves."

Elena sits beside me and pats my hand. "It's okay to be bothered by it, Maura. Just because you know about our world doesn't mean it's any easier to accept. It will take some time to process it, so don't rush it."

She reaches out and places a reassuring hand on my shoulder. "But if it's any consolation, remember that you're surrounded by people who will go to great lengths to protect you. Luk, our brothers, and me. You're part of this family now, and we take care of our own."

Despite Elena's reassuring words, I still feel a tightness in my chest, and panic takes hold of me.

My eyes brim with tears, and I feel a deep sense of shame at my inability to keep them at bay. "I'm sorry," I say to Elena, my voice trembling. "I shouldn't be crying. You must think I'm an emotional fool."

To my surprise, Elena doesn't dismiss my feelings or scold me for showing emotion. Instead, she gives me a knowing look and hands me a handkerchief. "It's okay to be scared and confused, Maura. Your world changed overnight. Don't be so hard on yourself."

Her kindness catches me off guard, and I accept the handkerchief, dabbing gently at my eyes. "I just feel so overwhelmed," I admit.

Elena watches me silently and patiently as I struggle to compose myself.

Slowly, the tears begin to subside, and Elena says gently, "I understand. But you'll get used to it."

I nod, taking in her words.

"For now," she continues, "just pay attention to what Luk says. He's the head of the family, and he knows what he's doing. And most importantly, never hide anything from him. In our world, secrets can be deadly. They can destroy trust, relationships, everything."

"I understand," I reply with a newfound determination. "No secrets."

Elena nods in approval, her smile reassuring. "You're stronger than you know, Maura. And you have a whole family here to support you. Remember that."

She looks at me thoughtfully, gauging my state of mind. "Do you want to go back inside? Or maybe," she suggests, glancing around the serene garden, "you should spend a little time out here by yourself. It's quiet and peaceful. The garden always has a way of comforting me whenever I'm feeling lost."

It's a good suggestion. "That sounds nice," I reply, feeling a sense of gratitude for her understanding.

Elena stands up, offering a final piece of support. "If you need anything, just find me," she says with a warm smile.

"Thank you, Elena," I say. "I really appreciate it."

As she walks away, I take a deep breath, but because I still feel a bit shaky, I decide to remain in the garden for a while, hoping it will have the same calming effect on me that it has on Elena.

Before long, however, my mind turns to Luk.

The thought of seeing him again fills me with conflicting emotions. There's not only the undeniable and intense physical attraction that I hadn't anticipated, but there's also a hesitancy, a reluctance to give in to the lust so easily. Although I understand what's expected of me as a wife, I don't want him to view me as a pushover, an easy lay. I want him to respect me, too, as an individual.

My fear is that I'll open up to him too soon, and he'll take advantage of my feelings. That could lead to my being hurt. And part of me wonders if I do share my emotions, concerns, and fears about being his wife that he won't be able to or even try to understand. He is deeply entrenched in a world of violence and power. How can I expect him to comprehend the complexities of my heart?

As I sit in the quiet of the garden, I realize that these are questions only time can answer.

CHAPTER 7

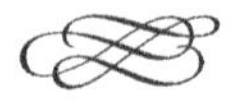

LUK

As I step into the somewhat rundown yet still luxurious apartment, Laurel greets me with her trademark blend of snark and false sweetness.

"Well, if it isn't Lukyan Ivanov gracing me with his presence? To what do I owe the pleasure? Or has the new bride already come to bore you?"

Laurel is a beautiful, Ivy League-educated princess who always knows just what to say to get under my skin. She's a brat and an entitled one at that, sharpened by the fact that, due to her family's financial ruin, her ambition to marry me and secure her future has been thwarted.

Before I can respond, Lev, standing just behind me, chuckles to make his presence known. "Careful, Laurel. Your claws are showing," he says, his voice laced with a cautionary edge.

Laurel's eyes flick over to Lev, and I can see her calculating, reassessing. Lev's reputation precedes him—his unpredictable nature and unmatched skills as an interrogator for the Bratva have made him a man you don't want to cross. She visibly reins in her attitude, offering a faint smile and waving her hand dismissively. "I'm just kidding, Lev. You don't need to be so serious all the time," she says, her tone smoothing over the earlier bite.

I watch the exchange silently, reminded of why my engagement to Laurel was doomed from the start. Her goal to marry into the Ivanov family for money and influence was clear, but it was the realization of her cunning nature that led me to end things. My marriage to Maura only sealed the deal.

"Let's get down to business and cut through the bullshit. We're not here for false pleasantries, and you damn well know it."

Laurel nods, the mask of sophistication back in place, as she gestures for us to take a seat. Unable to resist another jab, she leans forward with a smirk. "So, how's blissful married life with your beautiful new bride? It must be quite the change from the fun you used to have with me." She winks.

The comment hits a nerve, and I grit my teeth, feeling a surge of defensiveness wash over me. Maura is strong but innocent, and I fiercely want to—and will—protect her.

I lean in and lock eyes with Laurel. "Maura means more to me than you ever did. It's a shame you were never good enough for me even to consider marrying," I retort sharply.

The dig takes Laurel by surprise, momentarily silencing her. I'm not here to trade barbs with her, however. The real reason for my visit is the assassination attempt, and I decide to bait her into revealing any knowledge she might have about the attempt on Maura's life.

Watching her closely for any telltale signs of deceit, I say, "I'm sure you heard about what occurred during our wedding. Do you have anything you want to share about that?"

Laurel feigns a look of shock. "All I heard is that some guy tried to take out your bride. Quite a twist of fate, huh?" She forces a laugh, telling me she's lying. She knows more than she's saying.

I fix my gaze on her, trying to pierce through her evasiveness. "You're well-connected. You must have heard something that could help us."

Laurel meets my stare, her expression composed, a slight smile playing at the corners of her lips. "Luk, darling, you give me too much credit. I'm just a socialite these days. What could I possibly know about assassination attempts?"

Her nonchalance grates on me, but before I can press further, Lev, standing just a stride behind me, leans in, his patience clearly worn thin.

"Cut the shit," he interjects sharply. "We're not here to play games. Spill what you know—now. Your feeble attempts to deny it aren't working."

Laurel's posture stiffens, and she slowly reaches for her glass of champagne. "You've always had a way of getting straight to the point, Lev," she says, her voice dripping with disdain.

Taking a sip, her eyes narrow as she sets the glass down with more force than necessary. "You think I'm behind this, that I would stoop so low?" Her tone is laced with anger and a hint of betrayal.

I can't help but interject, driven by frustration and a need to confront the past. "Given our history, it's not a stretch to think you might hold a grudge. You clearly are pissed that I ended our engagement."

She looks at me with contempt. "Me, hold a grudge? Please, Luk, I'm so over you. But if you think I could have a hand in orchestrating something so vile, better think again."

Laurel reaches for her glass again. I can't help but note her extravagant drinking of champagne when I know she can't afford it, and the fact that she's day drinking doesn't escape me either.

"You were always a suspicious son of a bitch," she snarls. "Some things never change."

I meet her gaze steadily, unflinching. "Tell me straight, no games. Did you have anything to do with the assassination attempt?"

Laurel slumps as if defeated. "No," she states firmly, "I didn't have a damn thing to do with it."

She pauses, letting her words hang in the air before continuing, a bitter edge to her voice. "But after what you did to me..." Her sentence trails off as she gathers her thoughts, her gaze fixed on me with an intensity that's hard to ignore.

"You were supposed to be the savior of my family," she finally says, her voice low but laden with accusation. "That all went down the toilet when you rejected me. Assassination isn't my style," she adds, her tone defiant. "But there's no doubt in my mind that you're deserving of some sort of karmic punishment."

Her words cut deep, revealing the depth of her resentment and the pain caused by our broken engagement. But despite her bitterness and the accusations thrown my way, I find myself believing her when she says she had nothing to do with the assassination attempt.

I take another glance around her apartment, noting clothing, takeout containers, and empty champagne bottles strewn here and there. Laurel, in her current state, looks like she'd have trouble planning a trip to buy more booze, let alone masterminding an attempt on Maura's life.

Feeling a sense of closure on that front, I stand up, ready to put this uncomfortable situation behind me.

"I'm leaving," I announce, my tone final.

"Wait," Laurel calls out, a note of desperation in her voice.

I pause, half out the door, my instincts telling me just to walk away. Yet a part of me wonders if she might have some further information, something she's been holding back.

Lev, sensing my hesitation but ready to move on, nods at me. "I'll start the car," he says and steps out past me, leaving me alone with Laurel.

Once Lev is gone, Laurel shifts her approach dramatically. Gone is the angry, wronged ex-fiancée; in her place is a woman trying to exude a sexy, sweet demeanor. "Look, yes, I'm mad at you for dumping me," she starts, her voice softer, attempting to weave a seductive undertone into her words. "But that doesn't mean we can't come to another arrangement."

She closes the distance between us with a sultry sway in her step, her eyes alight with a predatory hunger.

Her suggestion takes me aback, and my confusion is evident. Laurel leans forward, deliberately unbuttoning one of the top buttons of her shirt to reveal a hint of cleavage. "If we can't be husband and wife," she says, her gaze locked on mine, "how about husband and mistress?"

Her proposal leaves me momentarily speechless. The audacity of it, the complete shift in her demeanor, is jarring.

"I've seen your Maura," she purrs, her voice dripping with insinuation. "No doubt she's a prude, Luk. She couldn't possibly give you what you *really* like." Her hand reaches out toward me in a provocative gesture below my waist, aiming to ignite a desire she assumes still lingers.

But I quickly avoid her touch and grab her wrist firmly, stopping her in her tracks. My grip is tight but controlled. "You should be grateful that all I did was dump you," I say coldly, my words laced with a warning as I push her hand away.

"I know you never had real feelings for me," I state flatly. "Your affair with Charlie Baird made that quite clear."

The mention of Charlie, a now ex-employee of Ivanov Holdings, leaves her visibly shaken. It's the first time I've seen genuine concern flicker across her face since I walked into her apartment. Her attempt at seduction falls away, replaced by sudden worry.

"Charlie?" she questions, her voice laced with apprehension. "I haven't heard from him in weeks. What happened to him?"

Her inquiry hangs in the air, but I choose not to satisfy her curiosity. Whatever fate befell Charlie Baird is not a matter I'm inclined to discuss with Laurel.

With nothing left to say, I turn and walk out the door.

CHAPTER 8

LUK

After a long day of fruitless inquiries and dead ends, I find myself back at the mansion. The sun has set, leaving the house bathed in the soft, silvery glow of moonlight that pours in through the tall windows. The vastness of the mansion feels more pronounced at this hour, with the staff gone for the day and the quiet enveloping every corner like a thick blanket.

I've always appreciated the tranquility that comes with this time of night. The house takes on a different character; it's almost castle-like. And in such moments, I can't help but feel like the lord of the castle, overseeing my domain in solitude.

The attempt on Maura's life still weighs heavily on my mind, a constant reminder of the dangers lurking in the shadows, threatening my new bride.

The stress clawing at my insides pushes me toward the bar. I pour myself a drink that matches the day's weight—something strong enough to dull the edge.

Leaning against the bar, I catch a glimpse of myself in a mirror. I look worn down, tension etched in deep lines on my face. My thoughts, relentless as ever, circle back to Maura. The realization of how close I came to losing her reignites a fury inside me, a raw, burning rage that's unexpected in its intensity.

How is it that a woman I barely know has burrowed so deep under my skin so quickly? What is it about her that stirs this fierce protectiveness, as if she were my own flesh and blood?

The more I dwell on it, the clearer it becomes: My urge to shield her isn't just about duty. There's something in Maura that resonates with me on a level I can't quite explain, a connection that's as real as the drink in my hand.

As I stand there, the alcohol barely taking the edge off, I'm forced to admit that Maura has changed the game for me. She's woven herself into the fabric of my life in an astonishingly short period.

Finishing my drink, I realize what I want, what I *need*, is unmistakable. I make my way up to the master bedroom. The room looks empty until I see her stretched on the bed, bathed in moonlight. The sight of her looking so serene is breathtaking—unexpected and powerful.

The moonlight casts shadows that play across the curves hidden beneath the covers, curves that stir a deep, primal longing within me. Her red hair is spread out across the pillow, a fiery halo around her delicate features, making her appear almost ethereal.

I stand in the doorway, caught in the moment, just looking at her. Seeing her lying there, so vulnerable yet so captivating, brings back a feeling inside me that I thought was long gone. Her presence softens me.

The pull toward her is too strong, an urge that's impossible to resist. Quietly, I slip out of my shoes and slide into bed next to her. It's a bold move, but something deep inside me craves the closeness, the simple comfort of being near her.

To my surprise, she instinctively eases into my embrace in her sleep, as if, even in her dreams, she knows I'm here to protect her. My arms wrap around her, pulling her closer, and I'm immediately struck by the warmth of her body against mine. It's a sensation that's new yet feels deeply right, filling me with a sense of peace I hadn't realized I was missing.

As she smiles in her sleep, my heart tightens at the sight. It's a simple, unguarded moment that I find utterly irresistible. The physical and emotional barriers between us seem to melt away in the quiet of the night.

When she finally opens her eyes, the surprise in them is evident. She gasps softly, the confusion of waking up to find me next to her written across her face. I can see the flicker of fear before she fully recognizes me, and it's that fear that spurs me to reassure her.

"Hey, it's okay," I say softly, my voice low and calming. "You never need to be afraid of me. I could never hurt you."

The words are a vow, a promise laid bare in the moonlit room.

When she finally speaks, her voice is vulnerable. "What happened at the wedding is still weighing on me," she admits, her words tinged with worry.

I nod, understanding all too well the shadow that incident has cast over us. "I know," I reply, my voice a soft rumble in the quiet of the room. "But I promise you, I will never let anything happen to you."

Despite the uncertainty in her eyes, Maura doesn't shy away. She stays close, her body pressed against mine. As I whisper reassuring promises that she's safe with me, I catch a slight parting of her lips, an unspoken invitation that hits me deeply.

The air between us crackles with equal parts desire and restraint. I lean in, my lips finding hers in a soft kiss that slowly ignites, passion flaring as we fall into a rhythm. My movements are measured, every caress laden with the raw need that's been simmering beneath the surface. Her heartbeat thunders against my chest, a mirror to my own racing pulse.

I slip my hand under her nightgown and over the flat plane of her belly, taking hold of her breast. She gasps as I touch her, those gorgeous eyes going wide with surprise. Her breast feels divine, her nipple small and pert, going hard against my touch.

Her initial expression of surprise soon turns to one of lust, her eyes closing as I continue to caress her. Maura's lips part slightly, her tongue running over them.

She pulls off her nightgown and tosses it aside, exposing her gorgeous breasts, her perfect belly, and her delicious hips. The animal need that I feel whenever I see her boils within, a knot that needs to be undone.

I want to give her more.

My hand drifts down. The coarseness of the hair just above her womanhood greets me, and I move over it to the warmth between her thighs.

She gasps again as I touch her. I love the position I'm in, her pleasure at my total control. It's impossible to resist leaning down and kissing her again, feeling her tongue flick against mine as she moans.

I spread her lips and tease her clit, her eyes opening and flashing again before wincing shut with pleasure. Maura's right where I want her, and I decide it's the perfect time to introduce her to my predilections.

To begin the process, I stop touching her, holding my hand still right over her sensitive nub. When she realizes what's going on, she opens her eyes slowly. Confusion paints her gorgeous features.

"Something wrong?"

"Not at all."

"Then why did you stop?" She bucks her hips up a bit as if trying to restart the process.

"Because now's as good a time as ever to lay down some ground rules."

"There are rules?"

I grin. "Informal ones, but rules nonetheless."

She licks her lips, her brow furrowing a bit, a playful gleam in her eyes. "What kind of rules?"

I move my hand over her belly as I begin to speak; her body is irresistible.

"I'm a man used to being in charge. That doesn't end in the bedroom. Here, between these sheets, you're mine. And you do as I say, understood?"

She lies still, her eyes wide, as if she doesn't know quite how to respond to what I've just told her.

I realize a little more clarification is in order. I decide to start simply, to ease her into it.

"Firstly, in the bedroom, my name is not Luk. It's Sir. Do you understand?"

She nods slowly. "Yes."

"Yes, *what*?"

"Yes, Sir."

My cock twitches at her words, the small step she's taken in giving herself over to me.

"Next, you only come when I say you can come. Is that understood?"

Her eyes flash. I can't quite tell if she's scared, excited, or a little of both.

"You want me to ask permission?"

I chuckle, reaching forward and taking her face in my hand. I lean in and kiss her hard, her lips parting, her tongue finding mine. I back away slowly, letting the kiss wash over her, allowing it to make the argument for me.

"That's exactly what I want."

She shudders, and I can tell that it's a shudder of delight.

"Take hold of me." It's a simple request, one to ease her into the process further. She complies, opening my belt and zipper and pulling down the top few inches of my boxer briefs. I'm as hard as it gets, my cock springing into her hand.

"Stroke me."

She does as I ask. Maura's slender fingers wrap around me, moving up and down, up and down. I close my eyes, focusing on her soft touch against my length.

"Good. Now, come here."

Without waiting for her response, I take Maura by the hips and pull her off the bed. She lets out a surprised squeal, one that I happen to find adorable, as I place her on the floor. I rise, looming over her, gazing down into those gorgeous eyes.

"I'm going to sit down in this chair," I say, sweeping my hand to the elegant wingback nearby. And I want you to get on your knees in front of me."

She nods.

"Then what?"

I grin. "No questions. You'll know what you need to know when you need to know it." She's a smart girl so I'm sure she's got some ideas.

I take my seat in the chair and stretch my arms out. She steps over, her gorgeous body sheened in silver moonlight.

When she's near, she gets on her knees before me.

"Now, take me into your hand again. Do what you were doing before."

She does, her eyes on mine as she grasps my cock, slowly working it up and down perfectly. But I want more.

I reach over and place my hand on her chin.

"Have you ever pleasured a man with your mouth?"

Her eyes flash. "No."

Knowing that I'm going to be yet another first for her sends a tingling thrill up my spine.

"Start by kissing the head."

Her eyes flick down to my cock, and I can sense she's already wondering how the hell she's going to fit all of me in her mouth. But she doesn't protest as she leans down, puckering her lips and kissing me where I ask.

The sensation of her lips on my end is perfect, sending electricity through my body.

"Now, open your mouth and take it in."

She gives a quick nod before she parts her lips slowly, wrapping them around my head. She's wet and warm, and the sight of her with me in her mouth is enough to make me feel like a goddamn beast.

"Keep going. Just like that."

I watch as she takes more of me into her mouth, moving up and down, her eyes locked onto mine.

"Does that feel good?" she asks, taking a short break, stroking me as she speaks.

"Does that feel good *what*?"

A whisper of a grin crosses her face. "Does that feel good, *Sir*?"

"Very. Keep going. You're a quick learner."

She returns to the task, wrapping me in her lips and moving up and down my shaft. The pleasure is insistent, starting from the base of my cock and rising slowly. Maura might be new to this, but there's no doubt that she could easily make me finish. The idea of erupting into her mouth, watching her swallow every last drop, is extremely tempting.

But I want more.

When I'm ready, I place my hand on her cheek and gently guide her off. My cock glistens from her work.

"Go over to the bed."

She does as I instruct, turning and walking over to the bed, her heart-shaped ass a magnet for my eyes.

"Now, bend over."

She does as I say, and I can see that she's already wet, ready for me. I stand, stepping over to her and taking her by the hips, barely able to contain myself. I take my cock by the base and place it at her entrance.

"Ask for it."

She squirms against me. "Please, Luk. Please."

"Please, *what*?"

"Please, *Sir*."

And that's all I need to hear. I push slowly, my length gliding into her effortlessly. She moans as I enter, her chest expanding and contracting as I push deep inside. She's so wet, her walls gripping me perfectly, her arousal making it clear how much she wants what I'm giving her.

I press my hips against her hard once I've bottomed out, giving her a moment to accommodate my size. Then I place my right hand on her gorgeous, round ass and raise it slightly, bringing it down with a sharp crack.

She gasps. When I take my hand away, there's a faint, red print.

"How does that feel?" I ask.

"It's... it's nice. Surprisingly so."

I do it again, watching her rear shake with the impact. Each connection pulls another sharp gasp into her mouth, her cheeks flushed with arousal.

"Oh... oh my God." The words pour out of her when I return to thrusting. I've given her enough of a sampling of my tastes, and now all I want is to make her come hard.

I buck into her, feeling her pussy clench around me, listening to the sounds of her moans fill the air. Her breasts sway back and forth, and the orgasm she'd nearly brought me to with her mouth is once more on the verge.

"I want you to come for me, Maura," I growl. "I can tell you want to. Come for me right now."

"Yes."

"Yes, *what*?"

"Yes, *Sir*!"

With one final scream, Maura comes. Her pussy grips me even harder, her ass pressed against me as she makes sure every inch of my length is inside as she comes. I join her, grabbing her rear and pushing into her one final time, my cock draining deep within her.

She falls onto the bed, and I join her. Without a word, she curls into my arms. Tenderness afterward is perhaps the most important part, and I make sure to give it to her.

I place a kiss on her forehead and watch as her eyes close.

We might be just getting started, but it was an excellent first lesson.

CHAPTER 9

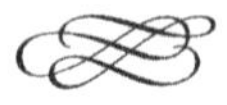

MAURA

"Lily, you seriously have the best gossip. How do you even keep up?" I chuckle, leaning back in my chair, completely engrossed in her storytelling.

Sitting in the sunroom two weeks later, the afternoon sun casting a warm, golden glow around us, I can't help but feel at ease with Lily. She's in the middle of dishing out the latest dirt, her tales a mix of the hilarious and the eyebrow-raising.

Lily grins, leaning closer as if she were sharing state secrets. "Oh, you know, walls talk, doors have ears, and I just happen to be at the right place at the right time. And apparently, the staff was all on the fence about you at first. New blood always gets the rumor mill churning."

I'm not surprised, but still curious. "Yes? And what's the word on the street now?" I ask, swirling my tea.

Her smile broadens, and it's clear she's pleased with the news she's about to share. "Well, the tides have turned,

Maura. Everyone's pretty excited that you're here. You've shaken things up in the best way possible."

I'm reassured to hear that, more than she might realize. "That's nice to know. I was a little worried I'd be the awkward new kid for a bit longer," I admit, feeling a genuine smile spread across my face.

Lily laughs, her gaze conspiratorial. "Awkward? Far from it. And if anyone gives you a hard time, they'll have to answer to me. I've got your back."

Her declaration, half in jest and half dead serious makes me laugh out loud: "Thanks, Lily. It's really nice to have you in my corner."

Leaning forward, Lily's eyes sparkle with a hint of mischief. "So, how are things going with the lord of the house?" she asks, her voice dripping with playful irony as she emphasizes the title.

Her question catches me off guard, and for a moment, I'm torn on how to answer. Talking about Luk behind his back feels like stepping into dangerous territory. Yet there's a part of me, perhaps emboldened by the growing camaraderie between Lily and me, that wants to share, to give voice to the whirlwind of emotions I've been navigating alone.

Lily, sensing my hesitation, nudges me gently, her curiosity clear. "Come on, you can tell me. What's he really like?"

I cave, a small sigh escaping me as I decide to open up. "Luk is... surprising," I start, choosing my words carefully. "At first, he seemed so cold, so untouchable. But there's this warmth, a kind of tenderness that I've started to see more of. It's like catching glimpses of sunlight on a cloudy day."

I pause, feeling both vulnerability and relief at sharing this insight. "And do you know what? I actually like it. I'm discovering a secret side of him that he doesn't show to the world."

Lily listens intently, a warm smile spreading across her face as I speak. Our intimate bubble is suddenly pierced by Svetlana, one of the service staff. She approaches with a respectful, albeit apologetic, demeanor. "I'm sorry for the interruption, Mrs. Ivanova, but you have a guest. Mrs. Sharon Halsey is here to see you."

Hearing Sharon's name sends a jolt of ice through my veins. She's finally rid of me; what could she possibly want now?

Lily catches the immediate change in my expression, her own setting into a mask of concern. She's nominally aware of the complex history between Sharon and me, the undercurrents of tension, and the potential for conflict. "Hey, you don't have to meet with her if you don't want to," Lily says quickly, her voice low. "This is your house, and you don't have to entertain anyone you don't want to. That's also the nice thing about having us around; we can keep away whomever you don't want to see."

I'm tempted by the offer, if only for a brief moment. The prospect of avoiding a confrontation with Sharon appeals to the part of me that's still rattled by the mention of her name. But the part of me that's been growing stronger and more determined since my wedding day knows that avoidance isn't the answer.

"No," I say, my voice firmer than I feel. "I need to meet with her. But thank you, Lily, really."

"All right, but if you need anything, just holler. I'll be around."

I nod, grateful for her support, and take a deep breath, steeling myself for the encounter ahead.

Stepping into the parlor, my heart is pounding in my chest, anticipation and dread swirling within me. Sharon is waiting for me with that all-too-familiar syrupy smile plastered across her face. She's dressed to the nines, as always, in something tight and clearly expensive.

Just one second in her presence and I'm already reminded of why I'm so grateful for my new life away from her. She was once a constant source of tension and manipulation, but that now feels like nothing more than a distant, unpleasant memory.

My stepmother doesn't waste any time. She hurries over with a speed that belies her usual composure, wrapping me up in a hug that's as bony and uncomfortable as I remember.

"Maura, darling, it's *so* good to see you," she coos, her voice dripping with artificial sweetness.

The hug, meant to convey warmth and affection, feels nothing short of performative. As she pulls back to appraise me, I'm reminded of the games and manipulations that Sharon plays all too well.

I don't waste any time. "What are you doing here, Sharon?" My tone is direct, cutting through the niceties.

She feigns hurt, dramatically placing her hands over her heart. "Oh, Maura, you wound me. Can't a mother check up on her daughter? Especially after such a whirlwind marriage and that dreadful attempt on your life."

Her words are calculated, each one laced with pretend concern. It's clear she's playing a part, but the sincerity is as thin as the smile plastered on her face.

"*Step*mother," I correct her as I've done so many times before.

My eyes drift to Rory, stationed like a statue near the doorway. It's enough to make me keep my guard up.

"I'm fine," I reply, keeping my response curt and to the point. "Luk is handling the investigation into the assassination attempt."

Sharon's reaction is theatrical, almost comical, in its intensity. "Oh, that's wonderful to hear!" she exclaims, a little too brightly, a little too eagerly. It's hard to tell where her true feelings lie beneath the layers of her over-the-top performance.

Sensing the undercurrent of something unspoken, I decide it's time to cut through the façade. "Sharon, let's get to the point. What's really on your mind? Why are you here?"

For a moment, she seems taken aback, her mask of overzealous concern slipping to reveal a glimmer of genuine emotion. It's a rare glimpse into the real woman, not often seen beneath her usual drama.

She sighs with a hint of resignation. "All right, Maura. You've got me. I do have other reasons for wanting to see you beyond checking in on your well-being. I wanted to discuss the matter of the inheritance."

I can't help but snort at the mention of the inheritance; my patience is already wearing thin. "You mean the money from my father that you managed to squander? Or are we talking about *my share*, which, let me remind you, you have no claim to?"

The tension in the room spiked, the mention of money casting a long shadow over our conversation. It was clear that despite Sharon's initial pretense of a familial visit, financial motives lurked beneath the surface, as they so often did with her.

Her demeanor shifted, her eyes narrowing as a wave of tense anger washed over her face. "Yes, I've used most of what your father left me," she admits through gritted teeth. "But it was all in the service of keeping the family business afloat. You can't possibly understand the sacrifices I've made."

I can't help but let out a sharp laugh at her justification. "No, I guess I didn't realize Louboutins and Birkin bags were crucial to our day-to-day business operations," I retort, my voice dripping with sarcasm.

Her response is quick and bitter, suggesting I've struck a nerve. "Maintaining appearances is important, Maura, as much as you might scoff at the idea. It's a part of the game we play; it's necessary to ensure that our position and influence remain unchallenged."

Sharon, seeing no way out, decides to lay her cards on the table. "I've burned through most of my share of the inheritance; it's true," she confesses, frustration and desperation etched in her voice. "And now, I need access to your portion to keep the Flanagan businesses above water."

I cross my arms, her plea leaving me cold. The idea of her squandering her share on luxuries and now eyeing my money is infuriating.

She continues, her tone earnest, "Maura, you have to understand. I can't just go out and get a loan. If our competitors—or worse, our enemies—catch even a whiff of our financial troubles, it'll be like blood in the water."

She pauses, looking me directly in the eyes. "There are other Irish families, powerful ones, waiting for a chance to snatch away everything the Flanagans have built in Chicago. Your father's legacy, our family's legacy, it's all at risk."

Her words, though self-serving, carry a weight of truth that I can't entirely dismiss. The precarious position of the Flanagan enterprises isn't news to me, but Sharon's direct plea, admitting her failures and desperation, puts the situation in a stark light.

However, her words fall on deaf ears. I stand firm; my resolve is unshaken. "I'm not interested," I assert, the newfound confidence in my voice surprising even me. "As far as I'm concerned, the Flanagan "legacy" as you call it, died with my father. And frankly, I'm more than happy to see it buried along with him."

Sharon's face contorts with frustration as she tries to sway me with more pleas of hopelessness, but I'm not having any of it.

"You can't do this, Maura," she says. "Think about your father; think about everything he worked for."

I cut her off, my tone making it clear there was no room for negotiation. "The matter isn't up for discussion,"

Turning away from her, I call out for Svetlana, who quickly arrives. "Svetlana, could you please bring two members of the security staff? It's time we escort my stepmother and her bodyguard to the front door."

Sharon looks taken aback, her schemes crumbling before her eyes. For the first time since her arrival, she's speechless, realizing she can't get her hooks into me any longer. As Svetlana nods and heads off to fetch the security staff, I feel a surge of empowerment.

Sensing the finality in the situation, my stepmother attempts to salvage some dignity. "There'll be no need for security," she says, her voice strained but composed. "Rory and I will leave without causing any trouble."

"I certainly hope that's the case," I reply, watching her closely. Despite her acquiescence, there's a sense of unfinished business lingering in the air.

As she and Rory make their way to the door, Sharon can't resist throwing one last barb my way. She pauses, turning slightly to toss a cryptic comment at me. "I'll be back, my dear. Just to make sure you're being a good little wife," she says with an ominous tone.

I watch silently as they leave, my gaze following them until they've left the mansion. Then, going upstairs to the second floor, I peer out the window, ensuring they're really gone.

Seeing them leave, I can't help but feel a surge of pride for standing my ground against Sharon. It was a confrontation I hadn't anticipated, but in facing it head-on, I'd taken an important step in defining my independence and embracing my new life.

However, even as the taillights of her car fade into the distance, I know deep down that this isn't the end. Her parting words, veiled in a sinister promise of return, infer that our paths will cross again. For now, though, I've shown that I won't be easily intimidated or manipulated.

CHAPTER 10

LUK

Days meld into one another, each passing in a blur of activity related to the vast network of Bratva operations under my control. I oversee the expansion of our territories, negotiating with precision and authority to secure new alliances while reinforcing old ones. I'm regarded in the city's underbelly with a mixture of fear and respect, a testament to the Ivanovs' reach and influence. Shipments come and go under the cover of night, their contents known only to a select few, each one adding to the Bratva's coffers and power.

But amidst the relentless pace of Bratva life, there's a parallel narrative unfolding—one that's quieter but no less significant. Maura is gradually finding her footing in the tumultuous world she's married into. I watch, often from a distance, as she navigates the complexities of our lives with a grace that never ceases to surprise me.

I know that she grew up in the business, but through observation and conversation, I am also aware that her father shielded her from the worst of it. While she came to me with a base understanding of the mob, the intricacies eluded her.

I see her in the garden, lost in thought among the blooms she's grown so fond of, or sharing a laugh with Lily, whose friendship has become a steady anchor in her new reality. There's a glint in her eyes, a sense of belonging that grows with each passing day.

Sitting across from Grigori in a nondescript coffee shop in downtown Chicago, the hum of the city a muted backdrop to our conversation, I find myself appreciating the normalcy of the moment. We're discussing the operational aspects of our business, the flow of arms, and the negotiations with suppliers—all the usual topics for us but the lifeblood of the Bratva.

Grigori, as always, is on top of everything. His attention to detail and knack for seeing the big picture ensures our operations run smoothly. "Everything's lined up for the next shipment. And the new routes are secure," he reports, his tone matter-of-fact.

I nod, taking a sip of my coffee. "Good work, Grigori. I always know I can count on you," I say, feeling a sense of pride in his unwavering competence.

There's a brief pause as he sets his coffee down, his gaze meeting mine with a level of understanding that comes from years of friendship. "I don't mean to pry, Luk," he begins, his voice taking on a more personal note, "but you know I can tell when something's on your mind. Spill it."

His directness doesn't surprise me. Grigori has always been able to read me like an open book, a skill that's both a blessing and a curse. I hesitate for a moment, contemplating how much I want to share.

Finally, I let out a slow breath. "It's nothing specific, just the usual challenges. Plus, there's Maura. She's adjusting, but I worry about the dangers. And then there's her stepmother, Sharon, lurking around with her own agenda."

"Yeah, that one's a real pain. Do you want me to get rid of her for you?"

I chuckle, a deep, rumbling sound that fills the small space between us. "Grigori, as much as I appreciate your direct approach to problem-solving, let's hold off on any drastic measures against her for now."

Grigori's smile doesn't waver; if anything, it grows wider. "Fair enough," he concedes with a light shrug. His gaze sharpens as he leans back in his chair, observing me with an intensity that feels almost too insightful. "You seem pretty smitten with your new bride."

I stiffen slightly at his observation, not out of displeasure but because it's a rare thing for me to discuss my feelings, even with someone as close to me as Grigori. I try to deflect, to keep the conversation from veering too far into personal territory. "Smitten? I'm not a lovestruck teenager."

But he isn't so easily deterred. With a playful, prodding tone, he pushes a bit more. "Come on. It's me you're talking to. You can admit it."

Caught in the gentle trap of his persistence, I relent, a small sigh escaping me. "All right, yes. I'm surprised myself, but I do like her, more than I thought possible," I admit, the words feeling strange yet true as they leave my mouth.

Grigori nods, a look of satisfaction settling on his features. "Good to hear. Arranged marriages can be hell on earth. But from what I've seen, yours is shaping up nicely. It's not often something genuine comes out of these deals."

My demeanor shifts, a shadow passing over my features as I contemplate his words. "There's something else," I confess. "Maura's guarded, especially when it comes to more intimate matters. I can't shake the feeling that she sees me as some sort of monster."

The admission feels like a weight has lifted, yet it lays bare my deepest fears. "I worry that she might run the first chance she gets if I'm not careful."

Grigori leans forward, his expression turning serious yet supportive. "You're being paranoid," he counters, a note of certainty in his voice. "From what I've seen, Maura's adjusting and perhaps even starting to like her new life. Give it time."

But my concerns run deeper, rooted in the darker aspects of my life and the person I've become. "That's just it, Grigori," I say, my expression turning grim. "All of that is contingent on her not knowing too much, of her not finding out about the *real* me, the things I've done, the blood on my hands."

The silence that follows is filled with the unspoken realities of our world, a world of violence and hard choices, a world that Maura—despite her strength and resilience—might never fully accept or understand.

Grigori studies me for a moment, his gaze thoughtful. "Don't underestimate her. You might be surprised," he finally says. "Maura's not like the others. She saw a glimpse of who you can become at the wedding when that asshole pointed a gun at her, yet she stuck around. Don't misjudge her—this could end up being everything you've ever wanted."

I know that his words are meant to reassure me, to offer a glimmer of hope in the face of my doubts. Yet the fear remains, a constant companion reminding me that the divide between Lukyan Ivanov, the Bratva commander, and Luk, the man who wants nothing more than to protect and cherish his wife, might be too vast for her ever to truly cross.

CHAPTER 11

MAURA

Wanting to take advantage of the beautiful spring day, I decide to take a walk through the neighborhood with my security detail trailing discreetly behind me. The sun is warm but not overbearing, a gentle breeze rustles through the budding trees, and the clear blue sky stretches endlessly above—it's the kind of day that breathes life into the city after a long winter. I find myself soaking in every moment, pretending, if only for a while, that I'm just another free soul out enjoying the day.

As I walk, my thoughts inevitably drift to the time I've been married to Luk. It's been a whirlwind of social functions and gatherings, each one a stage for me to play the role of the charming wife. Initially, the idea of being thrust into such a role made me bristle—being paraded around as some trophy didn't sit well with me. Yet, as I reflect on those experiences, I'm surprised to find that I kind of liked them.

Navigating these social waters is an art, a subtle dance of words and smiles, and I've found myself enjoying the challenge. The recognition and respect—even if some of it is borrowed from Luk's stature—have their own allure.

It's a far cry from where I thought I'd find happiness, but as I continue my walk, surrounded by the beauty of spring and the quiet presence of my security, I can't help but wonder if maybe this life with Luk could become more than just a role to play. Maybe it's a life I can learn to love, complexities and all.

My thoughts turn to a different set of memories, ones that cause my cheeks to color with warmth. The times Luk and I have shared in the privacy of our bedroom come to mind, each moment a vivid flash of intense passion, lust, and deep connection. There's an ease to losing myself in him, a profound surrender that I've never experienced before.

My independence has always been a cornerstone of my identity, yet there's something undeniably freeing about letting go, being vulnerable, and trusting him completely in our most intimate moments.

I think about our encounters and the playful exploration of each other's desires, and a shiver runs down my spine. It's a side of me I hadn't fully acknowledged until Luk, a depth of feeling and a capacity for passion that he's skillfully and gently coaxed to the surface. The way he respects my boundaries while simultaneously pushing them has opened a world of sensation I hadn't known I was missing.

I find myself biting my lower lip, a subconscious reaction as I replay those moments in my mind. The streets around me fade into the background as the memory of our closeness engulfs me, the heat between us, and the undeniable bond that is forming with each whispered word and shared breath.

Feeling overwhelmed and needing an escape from the tempest inside, I spontaneously decide to duck into a nearby florist. The moment I step through the door, the sights and smells of the shop envelop me like a comforting embrace. The fragrance of fresh flowers, the vibrant colors of blossoms in every hue imaginable—they all work together to soothe my frazzled nerves.

As I wander through the aisles, admiring the arrangements and the simple beauty of nature captured within the shop, my thoughts drift to what Elena said about the garden. I recall our conversations, her passion for the flowers, and how she's found peace and solace among nature. Surrounded by the floral scents and the quiet hum of the shop, I suddenly understand what she meant.

While enjoying my moment of tranquility, I am abruptly interrupted by a woman's voice. "Excuse me," she says. I look up, my eyes landing on a gorgeous, slender blonde with striking Slavic features. She is dressed in designer clothes from head to toe. There's an air of sophistication about her, yet something in her demeanor suggests a familiarity that's out of place in this setting. I inhale subtly and detect the faintest hint of champagne on her breath.

"Hi there. My name is Laurel," she introduces herself, her voice smooth and confident.

At the mention of her name, a gasp escapes me involuntarily. *Laurel.* The name resonates with a significance I wish I didn't recognize. She is Luk's ex-fiancé, the woman whose shadow has loomed—unspoken but ever-present—in the background of my new life.

Sensing my shock, Laurel offers a smile that's meant to be reassuring but comes across as menacing. "I know what you must be thinking," she begins, her tone attempting to convey sincerity. "But I'm here for a good reason: to warn you about Luk."

"Warn me? About *Luk*?" I manage to reply, my voice betraying curiosity and apprehension. "What could you possibly have to say that I want to hear?"

Laurel holds my gaze, a flicker of something unreadable in her eyes. "Oh, darling, you have no idea what you've gotten yourself into," she says, her voice condescending yet vindictive.

I'm torn between the urge to dismiss her outright and tell her to leave me alone and the suspicion that there's a depth to Luk I've yet to uncover nags at me fully. The line between loyalty and fear of the unknown is a precarious edge to walk.

Glancing over my shoulder, I note my bodyguards stationed outside. Their gazes diligently scan the street, oblivious to what's happening in the store. Because I have a momentary sense of privacy, I press Laurel for answers.

"What the hell are you talking about?" I demand, my voice low.

Laurel's response is a faint grin that makes my skin crawl. "Oh, Maura, I'm talking about Luk's... let's call them less conventional tastes in the bedroom," she says, her tone dripping with insinuation. "Surely, you know what I mean."

The implication hits me like a physical blow, leaving me at a loss for words. It's not just the accusation itself but the casual cruelty with which she delivers it, as if she's enjoying this, reveling in the discomfort she's causing.

"Is that supposed to scare me?" I ask, struggling to keep my voice steady. "Whatever Luk and I share is our business, not yours. We're fine," I assert, but the words feel hollow, even to my own ears. Laurel's smirk only widens at my response, as if she's scored a point in a game only she's playing.

Sensing the crack in my façade she leans in, her voice dropping to a conspiratorial whisper. "Oh, Maura, you really have no idea, do you? Luk's tastes can get much darker, much more dangerous than you might be prepared for," she says, her eyes locking onto mine with an intensity that's meant to unnerve me.

I want to dismiss her words, to tell her she's wrong, but doubt takes root in the back of my mind, growing with each syllable she speaks.

"I'm telling you this for your own good," Laurel continues, her tone softening slightly, but the underlying message is clear. "I know I'll never be with Luk again, but you need to be careful, to be on your toes. It can get nasty."

Before I can respond, Laurel straightens up, offering me a tight smile.

"Anyway, good luck, Maura," she says, her voice laced with a finality that sends a chill down my spine. With that, she turns on her heel and leaves.

I'm left reeling from the encounter. I went into the flower shop to seek quiet refuge, but what I got instead was an experience that left me unsettled.

In a rush to forget what has just happened, I quickly select a bouquet—lush peonies in soft pinks and whites intertwined with sprigs of eucalyptus and baby's breath—creating a delicate yet striking arrangement. Their beauty offers a brief distraction, but it's not enough to shake the uneasiness Laurel's words have inspired in me.

I hurry outside, barely making eye contact with the guards, as I tell them I want to go home. The walk seems endless as I replay the conversation with Laurel in my mind. Doubt and confusion churn within me, tainting my memories of moments with Luk. By the time we get back to the mansion, my thoughts are a tangled mess, and I'm desperate for solitude.

I retreat to my personal bedroom, seeking a quiet space to collect my thoughts and calm the turmoil inside me. However, the sight that greets me when I get there only deepens my confusion. On the bed lies a gift box, elegantly wrapped and unmistakably from Luk.

I approach and lift the lid. Inside, resting against a plush velvet lining, is a delicate lace collar accompanied by two equally delicate nipple clamps. The items are undeniably beautiful and crafted with care, yet the implications of the gift send a rush of heat to my cheeks.

I'm simultaneously intrigued and overwhelmed with a sense of shame—not because of the nature of the gift itself, but because I'm wondering what Luk will want me to do to thank him.

CHAPTER 12

LUK

Settled in the back of the car, I watch the lights of the city blur past as I make my way home after another grueling day of deal-making. Though exhausted, I grin to myself in anticipation of Maura's reaction to the gift I left for her. It was a bold move, one that's as much a test as it is a promise. We've been dancing around each other's desires, inching closer to a place where the barriers between us will become indistinguishable.

I'm convinced that I can guide her past her reservations to a place where she will fully embrace the depth of her submission, to the kind of surrender I see flickering in her eyes, the kind I know she's aching to give.

She's so close, her curiosity piqued, her body responding to my slightest touch, my every command. The gift is more than just an item; it's an invitation, a challenge.

The car pulls into the driveway, and I feel a sense of relief. Within the walls of the mansion, I'm not just Luk Ivanov, the Bratva commander with a reputation that precedes me.

I'm a man on the precipice of something transformative with a woman who's managed to carve a niche for herself in my world and my heart.

As I step out of the car, the anticipation builds. I'm certain Maura's reaction to the gift will be a turning point for us. It's a gamble, laying our desires out there so bare, but it's one I'm willing to take.

What we have, what we're building, is worth every risk. Tonight, I'll find out if she's ready to take that final step, to submit in the way we both crave.

I stride into the house, my steps quickening as I navigate through the familiar halls. There's an urgency in my movements, a keenness to see Maura, to gauge her reaction to my gift.

First, I check the garden, knowing that it's started to capture her interest. Not finding her there, I move on to the library, a haven for her where she can indulge in quiet moments. But she's not in either of her usual refuges.

Puzzled, I flag down one of the security guards passing by. "Have you seen my wife?" I ask, trying to control my impatience.

The guard nods, his expression neutral. "Mrs. Ivanova went to her personal bedroom upon arriving home about two hours ago, sir. She hasn't come out since," he informs me.

Wasting no further time, I head straight for her room, my pace quickening with every step. When I reach her door, a sense of foreboding tightens around my chest. I reach out, turning the handle, only to find it locked.

The locked door is an anomaly—a silent message that Maura is seeking solitude or perhaps that something more troubling is at play. Standing there in the dimly lit hallway, the anticipation and excitement that filled me moments before shifts to concern. I knock softly at first, then more insistently when I receive no answer.

"Maura?" I call out. "It's me. Are you in there?"

Although I can sense Maura's presence on the other side of the door, there's still no response, only heavy silence.

Frustration begins to simmer within me.

"Maura, talk to me," I call out, trying to keep my voice steady.

After a moment that feels like an eternity, she finally responds, her voice barely above a whisper. "I just need some time alone."

Her words halt my growing frustration, replacing it with concern. "Did something happen? I understand if you need space but shutting me out completely won't help us solve anything," I try to reason, hoping to bridge the gap her silence has created.

But she's firm in her resolve. "Please, Luk, just... not now."

As I stand there, my hand on the door handle, the urge to force the issue, to break through the barrier she's put up, is overwhelming. I'm torn between the desire to respect her wishes and the almost primal need to tear down the obstacles between us, to confront whatever has driven her to this.

Rage boils inside me like hot magma. I clench and unclench my fists, the door between us becoming the focus of my anger.

"Maura, open the door." My voice is even and calm but sharp as the edge of a razor.

Silence.

"Open the door right now."

More silence.

"Maura. Right. Now."

Still no answer.

Finally, I can't take it any longer. I raise my fist and slam it down hard against the thick wood.

"Maura! Open the door—*now*!"

No response. I slam my fist again and again. The door cracks a bit as pain shoots through my hand and into my wrist.

"You will open this door right now!"

The rage within me is a living thing, a ferocious, primal force I've spent a lifetime learning to control. Just as I'm wrestling with this inner turmoil, a familiar voice cuts through the haze of my anger.

"Luk," Grigori calls out, his voice grounding me. I look up to see him approaching, an expression of concern etched on his face.

He places a firm hand on my shoulder once he reaches me, a silent signal that it's time to step back and regroup.

"Patience," he advises.

My heart's beating hard, the rage still there, that monster I know all too well dwelling within. I turn my attention back to the door, feeling the urge to rip the goddamn thing off its hinges.

"Come, my friend," he says. "You're not doing yourself any favors."

He's right.

Heeding Grigori's counsel, I retreat to the sanctuary of my study, the anger simmering down to a low burn, replaced by a cold determination.

"Keep an eye out," I tell him, my voice now steady, "and stay nearby. I want to talk to her. Let me know the moment she comes out of that room."

Grigori nods, understanding the undercurrents of my request without needing further explanation. "You got it," he assures me before leaving me to my thoughts.

Alone in my study, the earlier fury gives way to a strategic calm. The need for patience becomes clear—whatever is happening with Maura, whatever barriers have risen between us, brute force won't tear them down. It's a game of chess, not war, which needs to be played.

As I settle into the silence, the resolve within me hardens.

But the monster is still there, his mouth curled up in a devilish grin. I know what he wants and what he'll do to get it.

CHAPTER 13

MAURA

I'm dreaming, lost in a world where only Luk and I exist. I'm ready and willing to explore the boundaries he's inviting me to cross and to discover new aspects of myself under his guidance.

He's standing over me, dressed in a suit with the tie undone, the top button of his collar open. He's like a statue, powerful and imposing, his gaze latched onto me. I'm tied to the bed, my wrists and ankles bound, my chest slowly rising and falling.

I'm his. Whatever happens next, it's Luk's decision.

I glance down at my breasts, the pinch of the nipple clamps insistent, with just the right amount of pain. The air is thick with anticipation.

Then, slowly, as if we have all the time in the world, Luk begins to make his way around the bed. His footfalls are heavy in the otherwise stillness of the room.

"You're beautiful," he says.

His words send a shudder of delight up and down my body. Despite my bindings, all I can think about is pleasing him. In a way, his enjoyment of my body makes *me* happy. Soon, he's at the side of the bed. He leans down until his lips are right over mine.

"You're going to come, and you're going to come when I tell you to. Understood?"

I want to kiss him. I want his touch. I want all of him more than anything. But he's keeping himself just out of reach, taking pleasure in depriving me.

"Understood."

He places his hand on the soft flatness of my belly, moving down, down over the red thatch of hair above my pussy. Then he reaches between my thighs, about to give me what I so desperately crave.

But then, abruptly, the fantasy shatters. I awake to the stark darkness of my bedroom, the remnants of the dream clinging to me like cobwebs. My hand, caught in the act of wandering below the waistline of my panties, freezes as the reality of my solitude sinks in. Embarrassment floods through me, hot and sharp, followed closely by a surge of annoyance.

I'm mad at myself, frustrated by my own body's betrayal and the vividness of my subconscious desires. The dream felt so real, so tantalizingly close to something I'm both curious about and afraid to embrace fully. Luk's gift, meant to be an exploration of trust and surrender, now feels like a taunt in the solitude of my room.

Sitting up, I push the feelings of embarrassment aside, trying to quiet the storm of emotions that the dream has unleashed. Longing, fear, and a burgeoning sense of self-awareness all meld together into something that I'm not entirely sure what to do with.

Alone in the darkness, my heart skips a beat as the silence of my room is pierced by an unsettling rustle from the corner. It's too dark to see, but the unmistakable sense of another presence sends adrenaline coursing through me. My breath catches, and I'm frozen, straining my ears for another sound.

Then, movement—a shadow shifts in the darkness. Panic flares up within me, but before I can scream, my instincts kick in. There's a figure lunging toward me, the silver of his blade glinting in the pale moonlight. Time slows down as I roll to the side, narrowly avoiding the attack. The figure, caught off balance by my sudden movement, stumbles forward.

There's a sharp pain in my arm—a reminder that the danger is real—but I don't have time to dwell on it. My survival instincts take over. I reach for the bedside lamp, throwing it toward the shadow in a desperate bid to disorient my attacker. The lamp misses, but the sudden burst it creates as it shatters against the wall gives me precious seconds to act.

I lunge for the heavy book on my nightstand, swinging it with all my might at the intruder. The impact sends them reeling back, and I scramble for the light switch. My heart is pounding, my breath ragged, and as the room fills with light, my attacker is revealed, dressed all in black.

The assailant covers his ears as I scream. The door suddenly bursts open, and Grigori rushes in. He's unarmed but, all the same, prepared for a fight.

The assailant turns his attention to the new face, seeing that a greater problem has arrived. The two square off against one another, both in fighting stances, ready to pounce.

Finally, the assailant makes a move. He lunges forward, stabbing at Grigori. For a moment, my blood runs cold as I worry his blade will find its mark. But Grigori is too quick for him. With one swift movement, he grabs the wrist of the attacker and twists. His knee follows upward, connecting with the man's forearm.

The collision is forceful enough to cause the attacker to drop his blade, which hits the floor with a clatter. Relief washes through me, but the fight's not over. Once the attacker's advantage is neutralized, Grigori slams his fist hard into the assailant's jaw. Another punch connects with his stomach, and that's all the man can take. He drops to his knees, and Grigori quickly restrains him.

"Get in here, you idiots!"

Two guards rush into the room, restrain the attacker with zip ties, and carry him out.

"I'll deal with him later," Grigori says matter-of-factly.

Once the intruder is dragged out of the room, Grigori turns his full attention to me. His approach is quick but measured, his concern evident in the set of his jaw and the intensity of his gaze. The adrenaline that had fueled my survival instincts just moments ago begins to wane, leaving behind a cocktail of emotions—relief, shock, and an unsettling realization of how close I came to real harm or possibly death.

"Are you all right?" Grigori asks, his voice carrying a depth of genuine concern. He scans me for any signs of injury, his presence a comforting solidity in the wake of unexpected chaos.

I nod, still trying to process what just happened while dealing with the aftereffects of the adrenaline surge. "Y-yes, I think so," I manage to say, my voice steadier than I feel. The reassurance that I'm physically unharmed does little to quell the internal turmoil, fear, and vulnerability that lingers.

He glances at my arm, and I suddenly notice a red slash mark. I barely register it, the adrenaline still in charge of my reactions.

"You're hurt," Grigori says.

"It's nothing. Really. I don't even feel it."

He snorts, "Not right now, you don't. Luk is not going to like this—not one bit."

CHAPTER 14

LUK

Anger courses through me as I march down the hallway, each step heavy with self-inflicted fury simmering within. How could I have allowed myself to become so ensnared in the trivial aspects of my work, isolating myself in my study, far from where I truly needed to be? The fact that I wasn't there for Maura when she needed me ignites a storm of self-criticism within me.

Catching sight of Grigori stationed near Maura's door brings a momentary pause to the raging storm within. Deciding to put him on watch, to alert me the moment Maura emerged from her room, now strikes me as the best single piece of foresight in a fog of errors. The wave of relief at this realization is tangible, momentarily cutting through the anger.

The chilling "what ifs" loom ominously, threatening to pull me into a vortex of grim possibilities I refuse to entertain fully. I forcibly dismiss these thoughts, focusing instead on the present relief, thankful for Grigori's vigilance in my absence.

I walk quickly, my gaze scanning him for any signs of injury. He's unscathed, thank God. Without wasting a moment, I demand, "I need to see Maura."

Grigori hesitates, a flicker of protest crossing his features, but I'm already moving past him, propelled by the need to see her with my own eyes and to confirm she's safe. I push open the bedroom door, my heart hammering in my chest with fear and urgency.

"Luk, I don't know if that is a good idea," I hear him say as I enter the room.

The sight that greets me is one of relief and tension in equal measure. Maura is there, and so is Elena, a scene that's comforting yet fraught with unspoken questions. "Are you okay?" is the first question I manage, and it tumbles out on its own, laced with concern that is resonating deep within me, a vulnerability I'm not accustomed to revealing.

Elena stands when I enter. She approaches me, placing a hand gently but firmly against my chest, a silent command for restraint. "Pause, Luk," she says, her directive resonating with empathy and authority.

I comply with Elena's request, my body calming under her tender touch. I stand there, my gaze instinctively searching Maura, taking in every detail of her physical state. She's visibly shaken, a vulnerability in her eyes that I've seldom seen. It strikes a chord within me, causing a deep, aching sadness. Worse still, I notice the tension in her body seems to be amplified by my presence, a realization that cuts deeper than any physical wound ever could.

My eyes catch sight of the bandage on her arm. A visceral rage surges within me at the thought of her being hurt, an emotion so potent it feels like it could consume me from the inside out.

Elena seems to sense the growing storm within me. With gentle but insistent guidance, she leads me away from Maura and out into the hallway. The space feels colder and emptier without Maura's presence, and I ache to be near her.

"She was hurt, but it's just a flesh wound that won't require stitches," Elena explains with an undercurrent of serious concern once we're outside of the room. "Right now, what Maura needs is calm, something that you are unable to provide given your current state."

The words sting, but I know she's right. The simmering anger inside me begins to subside.

"Stay with her, please. Get her anything she needs," I instruct, my voice steadier. I am warmly grateful for Elena's unwavering support.

Elena nods, her determination clear. "Of course. I'll keep you updated," she assures me before slipping back into the room and closing the heavy door that once again separates me from Maura.

I stare at the door for a moment longer, reciting a silent vow to do better, to be what Maura needs in the wake of this ordeal. I turn to Grigori, finding a sense of purpose in taking back control. "Double the security," I command, the need for action to ensure this never happens again taking precedence.

Grigori meets my purposeful gaze, his expression solemnly agreeing. "Already done. More men are on their way; they'll be here within the hour," he responds.

As we stride down the hallway together, the air between us is charged with anger, tension, and confusion. "Talk to me, Grigori. What do we know about the attacker? Who is he? And how the fuck did he get into my house?" I ask, eager to understand the assailant who dared to breach the safety of our home and put Maura in danger.

Grigori's response comes with a hint of a grin, a flicker of satisfaction in his eyes. "We caught him alive. The guards are taking him downstairs as we speak, preparing him for a little personal time with you," he says, the implication clear. The idea of facing this intruder head-on, of extracting the information we need directly, sparks a grim sense of satisfaction within me.

The notion of interrogation carries with it a weight of responsibility and a chance for retribution. It's a critical opportunity to gain insight into how we were breached and to learn how we can prevent any future attempts against us. Yet, as these thoughts solidify, the moment is shattered by the sudden ring of Grigori's phone.

He answers swiftly, his demeanor shifting from ambiguous to alert as he listens to the voice on the other end. I watch closely, noting the change in his expression and the sudden sharpness in his gaze. When he hangs up, the news he delivers cuts through the hallway's previously charged atmosphere like a cold blade.

"The assailant has escaped," Grigori reports, his voice tight with frustration and disbelief. "He took out one of the guards that was escorting him. But he's still on the grounds."

We sprint down the hallway, urgency fueling our every step as I press Grigori for more details. "Where is he?" I demand, my voice a low growl of barely contained anger and concern.

"Near the garden," Grigori replies, his tone just as biting. Our eyes scan ahead as we navigate the mansion's labyrinthine corridors, each turn bringing us closer to our target.

The pounding in my chest is relentless, a cacophony of adrenaline and determination as we burst through the final door. The cool night air greets us with a sharp bite. The garden looms ahead, bathed in the soft glow of moonlight, a serene location suddenly transformed into a battlefield.

Amidst the eerie calm stands the assassin, cornered but defiant, a half-dozen of my security team already in position, their firearms drawn and aimed with deadly precision. The unknown man, in a desperate bid for survival or perhaps sheer defiance, reveals his own gun, a sinister grin splitting his face like an evil jack-o'-lantern. From across the garden, I watch as he turns his attention toward me.

Time seems to slow, every detail sharpening under the moon's watchful eye. I'm about to shout to my men to hold their fire, to take him alive. We need his intel—we might be able to find out who sent him and understand the depth of the threat against us. But the situation quickly escalates beyond any chance of shouting commands, the assassin's next move triggering a silent, deadly standoff.

Shit.

Without warning, the man raises his gun.

"No!" I shout, desperate to prevent what I know is going to happen next.

But it's too late. My security detail opens fire. Gunshots begin popping off in the dark, orange flashes flickering across the garden, the smell of gunfire replacing the sweet scent of the beautiful blooms.

"Enough!"

The guards stop firing at once. As expected, the assassin is dead and lying in a heap on the ground.

There is a hushed silence; the only sounds are the soft night breeze and the collective, subdued breaths of my security team. With the immediate threat neutralized, I approach the downed man cautiously, my senses still heightened from the adrenaline rush.

Kneeling beside him, I examine him closely, searching for any clue that might reveal his motivations and affiliations. It's then that I spot it—a tattoo barely visible on his inner wrist beneath the sleeve of his dark attire. It's a Celtic cross, intricately designed, its lines sharp and deliberate. It's not just any tattoo; in our world, symbols like these are more than mere decorations. They connote allegiances and declarations and are symbols of honor.

A new resolve takes hold of me. The Celtic cross tattoo is a lead—a tangible piece of evidence in the shadowy world of loyalties and betrayals that define our existence. It's a clue that could unravel the mystery of who dared order someone to invade my home and threaten the person I hold most dear.

Turning to Grigori, I see the same realization reflected in his eyes. "This isn't over," I state, the weight of my words heavy with promise and vindication. "This tattoo, it's a clue that could lead us directly to who's behind this."

I won't stop until I find them.

But first, I need to see my wife.

CHAPTER 15

LUK

Grigori, Lev, and I sit across from Declan O'Leary in the dim light of O'Malley's, a traditional Irish pub, where there is a faint smell of aged whiskey in the air. The place has an authentic feel, with dark wood paneling and stained-glass windows casting colorful patterns on the floor. The din of muted conversations and laughter surrounds us. It's the kind of place where deals are made, and secrets are traded over a pint of good Irish stout.

We have come for answers, and I waste no time cutting to the chase.

"Declan," I begin, "we've got a problem. Another assassination attempt on my wife—*at my home*, no less—and all signs point back to the Irish mob."

Declan, with his easy smile and a twinkle in his eye, plays the part of the congenial host to perfection. But I'm not fooled. Behind that friendly façade lies a mind as sharp and as dangerous as any blade. Declan is the head of the O'Leary crime family and is known for his brutality as much as his business acumen. A man doesn't rise to the top of Dublin's underworld by being nice.

Declan leans back, feigning surprise, but there's a calculating look in his eyes. "Luk, my friend," he responds in his heavy Irish brogue, "that's a serious accusation. You know I'd never sanction such a thing against you."

I lean forward, locking eyes with him. "Maybe it didn't come from you but it was a member of an Irish mob, no doubt about it. There was a Celtic cross tattoo on his wrist. Ring any bells?"

There's a brief flicker of recognition in Declan's eyes before he attempts to mask it by taking a sip of his drink. "There are many with such tattoos," he says noncommittally. "It's a popular symbol."

I notice the subtle shift in Declan's demeanor; his casual dismissal sparks a surge of anger within me. My voice takes on a darker, more menacing tone. "Popular or not, someone's using it to mark targets on my back."

Lev places a reassuring hand on my shoulder, a silent plea for restraint. I take a deep breath, fighting against the primal urge to unleash violence in retaliation for the threat against Maura. The very thought of anyone daring to harm her ignites a fury in me, a desire to tear through the city until I find the responsible party.

Declan watches the interplay with a hint of amusement in his eyes, seemingly entertained by the display of raw emotion. Yet, as the conversation progresses, he adopts a more serious tone. "Luk, the man wasn't one of mine," he asserts, a note of sincerity in his voice that I begrudgingly accept as truth. "But I'll keep my ears open. If anything comes up, you'll be the first to know."

There's a moment where our gazes lock, an unspoken understanding passing between us. Despite the undercurrents of rivalry and the brutal nature of our world, there's respect, a silent recognition of the lines we don't cross. I nod, the tension easing slightly. "Thank you, Declan. I appreciate it."

With that, we take our leave. The weight of the conversation lingers in my mind as we exit the pub.

Stepping out into the cool embrace of a drizzly, gray afternoon, the city's mood mirrors my own—unsettled and brooding. We get into our car, and the hum of the engine provides calm as we move farther away from the pub and the discussion within.

As we weave through the streets of Chicago, I catch a glimpse of the skyline, a jagged silhouette against the overcast sky. It's a city of contrasts, of power and vulnerability, much like the delicate balance of our own lives within its shadowy limits.

Lev and Grigori break the silence, their voices a low rumble in the confined space of the car. We dissect the meeting, poring over Declan's words and judging his sincerity.

"Do you think he was being straight with us?" Lev asks, skepticism lining his tone.

I let the question hang in the air for a moment as I consider Declan's parting words. "Declan's tough, no doubt, but he's not a fool. He knows well enough that if we wanted to, the Bratva could crush his family without a second thought," I respond, a stark reminder of the power at our command and the threats that lace our interactions.

My confidence in Declan's truthfulness doesn't stem from trust, per se, but from a mutual understanding of the consequences of betrayal. Yet despite his assurance, the mystery of the Celtic cross tattoo nags at me. It's a symbol that points unmistakably to a connection within the Irish underworld.

Our discussion is abruptly interrupted by the buzz of my phone. A text lights up the screen. The contents shifts my focus, providing a new piece of information, perhaps a new lead.

The text is from a contact within the Mancuso crime family, offering to meet with me. I glance up from the screen, meeting Lev and Grigori's expectant looks.

"We've got a lead. The Mancusos are willing to talk," I declare. I've already decided that we will listen to whatever they have to say. We're diving deeper into the underworld's intricacies, and every piece of information is a weapon in its own right.

We direct the driver toward Little Italy, a neighborhood where the scent of authentic Italian cuisine fills the air, and old-world charm masks the modern machinations of crime syndicates.

We pull up to a restaurant that appears to be one of modern elegance. Its windows are darkened, a sign indicating it's closed for lunch but we know it is a front. We enter, our footsteps echoing in the quiet, tastefully decorated space.

At a booth in the corner, Vic Mancuso, the picture of isolation and control, sits. He's a man who effortlessly carries his power and his presence is commanding even as he awaits our arrival. His thick, salt-and-pepper hair is swept back from his ruggedly handsome face and his dark eyes are sharp, missing nothing. Dressed in a tailored suit that speaks of wealth and taste, Vic cuts a figure that's at once imposing and charismatic, a lion in his den.

As we approach, his gaze lifts to meet ours, a flicker of interest crossing his features. "Luk," he says, greeting me with a shady smile. His voice is smooth, with the hint of an Italian accent coloring his words. The tone is warm, but the underlying steel is there—a reminder that in our world, friendliness is often a mask for strategy.

I nod, taking the seat opposite him, Lev and Grigori flanking me. "Vic," I acknowledge, using an equally measured tone. "You said you had information," I add, getting straight to the point.

Mancuso's outward demeanor is warm, his hospitality almost disarming, but I'm well aware of the man's reputation. His hands are stained with more blood than Declan's. I don't let my guard down for a second.

Leaning forward, I pull up a photo of the would-be assassin on my phone, sliding it across the table toward him. As if on cue, thunder rumbles outside, and the rain begins to pelt against the restaurant's windows.

Vic takes a moment to study the image, his expression unreadable. Meanwhile, he gestures toward the array of food platters on his table, a spread that looks more suited for a banquet than a lunch for one. "Where are my manners?" he quips, waving his hand and offering us food and drink.

Lev starts to voice his interest but I cut him off with a sharp look. "Thank you, but we're here strictly for information," I state firmly, redirecting the conversation back to the matter at hand.

I lean in further, lowering my voice. "You're known for your extensive network, Vic. Your access to intel is unmatched," I begin, my tone indicating that I want to dispense with the pleasantries. "And let's not forget your past connections to the Flanagans." The mention of Maura's family name hangs heavily between us, a clear signal that I'm aware of the depths of his involvement in the city's underworld dynamics.

Vic sets down his wine glass, and his gaze sharpens at the mention of the Flanagans. The convivial atmosphere shifts subtly, an uncomfortable tension almost visible in the air. It's clear that we're venturing into territory where alliances and old loyalties are as complex as the network of streets in Chicago itself.

His confusion is clear, his brow furrowing as he tries to piece together the relevance. "Why the interest in the Flanagans, Luk? That's your wife's family, right?"

"Yes, it is," I confirm, my voice steady, betraying no undercurrent of the personal stakes involved.

Vic shrugs nonchalantly, the wineglass paused at his lips. "Truth be told, the Flanagans are not what they used to be. They had their time in the sun, but when the old man passed, it all but evaporated." He takes a sip of his wine, savoring the taste before continuing. "There was chatter at one point about Maura stepping up. She always was a bright girl. But as time went by, it seemed like she didn't want any part of it."

He sets his glass down again, his gaze drifting off as if recalling the details. "And Sharon," he adds, a slight smirk playing at the corners of his mouth, "she sure loves the spotlight and the power that comes with being in charge. But acumen? That's a different story. She's all show. She's got no real depth when it comes to running things."

Vic's words paint a picture I'm all too familiar with. The Flanagans, once a name that commanded respect and fear in equal measure, were now a shadow of their former glory. Maura's disinterest in taking the reins is something I've known and respected, and Sharon's superficial grasp on power is a detail that doesn't surprise me in the least.

"What about the Halseys? Sharon's lot?" I press. My voice is hard and demanding.

Vic can't help but laugh, a derisive sound that tells me all I need to know before he even speaks. "The Halseys? They're nothing. A smaller fall from grace compared to the Flanagans', but a fall nonetheless." He shakes his head, taking another leisurely sip of his wine. Sharon thought she was stepping up when she married into the Flanagans. She dreamed it would be her ticket to the big leagues."

He leans back, his smirk widening as he continues: " The Halseys have been easy to push around since Sharon's old man passed. But that Sharon... she's somewhat of an unknown. She's power-hungry, no doubt about it. And when power-hungry people get their taste, they don't step away from it so easily.

"The point is," Vic adds as his eyes lock onto mine, his tone more serious, "everyone fears the Bratva. The Italians, the Irish—everyone. No one in their right mind would go after a Bratva bride on her wedding night. It's not just bad for business; it's a death wish."

I lean back in my chair. "Everyone fears the Bratva, huh?" my voice is sharp like a blade. "I hope that includes you."

Vic's laughter rings out, a sound of confidence rather than defiance. "Yes, Luk, I know where I stand in the pecking order. I like my place and have no interest in stirring up trouble. I've got a cozy operation running."

He meets my gaze with a newfound seriousness. "And that's why I'll be the first to let you know if there's chatter."

"Good," I reply, the single word heavy with intent. "Because I'm going to get to the bottom of this. And I'll remember who helped me—and who didn't." The threat hangs in the air, its effect immediate. Vic's demeanor shifts, a touch more compliant, a subtle nod acknowledging the power dynamics at play.

As we stand to leave, Vic calls out to one of his men. "Bring out a crate of that fine Brunello di Montalcino for Mr. Ivanov as a token of my gratitude."

As we leave the restaurant, Vic's assistant follows with the crate of wine. We reach our car and get in as the crate is loaded into the trunk. The rain—cold and relentless—seems an almost fitting reflection of the path that lies ahead: dark, uncertain, and fraught with danger, but a path I'll navigate with the full force of the Bratva at my back.

Vic's cooperation and his willingness to share what he learns is a start. But in the grand scheme of things, it's just one piece of a larger puzzle.

Someone dared to target my family, to disrupt the fragile balance of power with a bold, calculated move.

And for that, they'll answer to me.

CHAPTER 16

MAURA

I have two secrets I am holding onto—ones that could ultimately change everything. The first is that I know more about the hitman than I've let on, juicy intel that I've been withholding, waiting for the right moment to reveal.

The second? I'm going to sneak out, and nobody will be the wiser. It's the perfect afternoon for an unauthorized adventure, and with Luk out for the day, there's no chance of him catching wind of my little escapade.

Two months have passed since the whirlwind wedding, moving into the mansion, and taking on the role of Luk's wife. At times, I feel like a caged songbird, and I need to get some air, stretch my legs, and remind myself what freedom feels like, even if for only a little while.

"I'll be taking a long bath, then a nap. I'm feeling a little under the weather and wish to be left alone," I tell the staff, my voice dripping with feigned weariness. They buy it, nodding sympathetically, completely unaware of the plot I'm hatching.

I've been watching the guards closely, learning their patterns and routines, and now, armed with this knowledge, I'm ready to make my move. I call an Uber, instructing the driver to pick me up on a side street down the block from the mansion. Once my transportation is set, I get dressed, grab the small handbag I've prepared, quietly leave my room, and make my way downstairs.

The timing has to be perfect. When one guard rounds the corner and another momentarily disappears inside, I seize my moment. My heart is beating a little faster, not from fear but from the sheer thrill of defying the intricate security measures designed to keep me safe.

As I sneak across the property, every step perfectly calculated, I'm overcome by the feeling of freedom. It's been ages since I've been able to blend in with the city anonymously. Thinking about the information I've received about the assassin, I can't help but feel like I'm holding onto a ticking time bomb. But for now, this is *my* little adventure, my middle finger to danger.

I reach the Uber and get into the back seat, telling the driver to go quickly. We take off, driving away from the mansion, and soon, I feel the city's energy pulsing around me. It's like I'm rediscovering a piece of myself that was buried beneath Sharon's strictness, the unexpected wedding, and the double-assassination attempt. I'm still on high alert, however, so I'm in disguise. I wear a Cubs cap and jersey, black-rimmed glasses, faded jeans, and Converse sneakers. I want to look like anyone but Maura Ivanova.

I head back to my roots—Bridgeport, the old neighborhood steeped in Irish culture. The walls of the houses here hold stories told by generations, and the smell of fresh bread mixes with that unmistakable hint of peat smoke, pulling me back in time.

I instruct the driver to stop and get out. The familiar streets wrap around me like a warm hug. But it's St. Brigid's Church that's calling me. It stands proud and inviting at the end of the block. It's more than just a building, it's a piece of my history, a silent witness to the highs and lows of my family's life, a teacher who never stopped teaching.

The sight of St. Brigid's stirs mixed emotions in me—nostalgia, longing, and a touch of mourning for the simplicity of the days spent within its walls. But I'm not there to reminisce; there's a purpose to my visit, a need to connect the dots of my past to the dangers of my present.

Stepping inside the church, a familiar air surrounds me, dense with the scent of incense and polished wood. Sunlight filters through stained glass windows, casting vibrant patterns across the stone floor, each ray illuminating scenes of saints and biblical tales.

I spot Father Samuel McCarry near the altar, his back to me as he tends to the candles. He's aged since I last saw him, his once dark hair now a silvery gray, but still, there's a vigor in his movements. He wears clerical clothing under a vestment, the outer fabric hanging loosely on his frame.

"Father McCarry?" I call out softly, not wanting to startle him.

He spins around, and in an instant, recognition clicks in his eyes.

"Maura? Maura Flanagan?"

As we share a long embrace, it feels as if no time has passed at all, even though it's been ages. I'm reminded of the times I'd run to him for advice or when I just needed someone to talk to. "Father, can we chat in your office? There's something I need to talk to you about," I tell him, trying to keep my voice steady.

"Of course, Maura, follow me," he says, a worried expression clouding his face. His office is nothing fancy—a desk drowning in paperwork, multiple religious, psychology, and mental wellness books filling the shelves, and a large photo of the current pope gracing one wall.

Sitting down across from Father McCarry, I suddenly find myself tongue-tied. The seriousness of why I want to speak with him hits me all at once. He leans in with concern and readiness to help. "What's on your mind, Maura? Are you looking for advice or is this more of a confessional visit?" he asks gently.

Part of me wishes I was there for confession, to offload some guilt. "Actually, Father, it's something else altogether," I manage to say. "I've got something to show you, and it isn't pretty."

He looks worried again, the lines around his eyes appearing deeper. "What's going on?" he asks, bracing himself for unsettling news.

Taking a deep breath, I dive into it. "It's about a death, Father. Of someone whom we know." Just saying it out loud makes the whole thing feel more real, heavier somehow.

Father McCarry straightens, a visible tautness to his posture as he prepares himself for what I'm about to reveal. "Go on," he says, a quiet strength in his voice.

I sigh as I pull out my phone, scrolling to the photo I want to show him. Taking it was a risk but also a necessity, driven by the need for answers. The image of a dead man, taken in the dim lighting of the basement, fills the screen. I hand the phone to him, my heart pounding. "Does this man look familiar?" I ask, watching his face for any sign of acknowledgment.

Father McCarry takes my phone with steady hands. As he examines the photo, a flicker of something casts over his eyes. I am unsure what, but recognition and a bit of shock come to mind.

This photo is the reason I've come to see him. Beyond seeking guidance or absolution, I need his insight, his knowledge of the community I've been away from for so long.

The silence stretches between us as he studies the photo, anticipation enveloping me like a glove.

Father McCarry's reaction unravels slowly, a realization creeping into his expression with a gravity that pulls at my heart. "That's little Sean McManus," he says, the weight of his words heavy with anguish. "Although he isn't so little anymore. What is this, Maura? What happened? And why do you have a photo of his body? I didn't even know he'd passed."

I take another deep breath, the air in the office suddenly feeling thick. "Father, there was an attempt on my life. Sean was the would-be assassin." The words feel surreal as they leave my mouth.

Father McCarry's expression of sadness deepens, but there's also a resignation there, an acknowledgment of a path long feared. "He was full of potential but troubled, always drawn to the shadows and trying to fit in."

"Remember the two of us in choir practice? And all the stupid stuff we used to do around here when we were kids?" I toss out there, trying to keep my voice light despite the lump in my throat.

Father McCarry's expression softens, a sad smile flickering across his face. "Oh, yes. The kid had a voice that could make the angels jealous. He sang those hymns like he was trying to reach heaven itself. It's hard knowing that's the same person in the photo you just showed me."

I let out a little laugh, the kind that recognizes a happy memory in sadness rather than anything funny. "Right? He'd always act so tough, but then he'd start singing, and we'd get a glimpse of the real him for just a bit."

The room grew quiet as we both took a minute to remember Sean as he was. Father McCarry looked down, his voice dropping a bit. "I tried to help him after things went sideways at home; I thought maybe this place could be his safe space. But you know how it is—once the streets get a hold of you, they don't let go very easily."

"Yes," I nod, remembering. "You did everything you could. But sometimes people are unreachable, unfortunately."

Father McCarry looks genuinely upset as he says, "Sean was one of our own. It's like we lost a piece of this place when he left."

"I agree," I say, feeling that same loss heavy in my chest. "But somewhere, somehow, he slipped through the cracks and got lost, unable to find his way back."

We both sit in silence for a moment, lost in our thoughts, the room feeling like a little bubble away from the rest of the world. "We've got to figure out why, Father. For Sean. He deserves that, at least," I say, feeling a new determination rising inside me.

Father McCarry looks up, his eyes meeting mine, and I see a fire there. "Indeed. For Sean and the kids like him. It's the least we can do."

Then, almost as an afterthought, he touches on Sharon and the shift in the neighborhood dynamics. " Nothing's been the same since Sharon took over the Flanagan operations," he remarks. "The balance has been off, and the community is suffering because of it."

"How do you mean?" I ask.

Father McCarry leans slightly forward, his voice dropping to a confidential tone as if the very walls of his office might be listening, ready to betray him. "Maura, what I'm getting at when I say Sharon has changed the neighborhood is not just about the power shift. There's a palpable difference in the air now—less trust, more suspicion."

I raise an eyebrow, intrigued yet saddened by his observation. "What exactly do you mean, Father?"

He nods to himself, a sigh escaping as he begins. "Well, for starters, there used to be a sense of honor among families, even those involved in... let's just say less savory activities. There were lines you didn't cross, unspoken rules that kept the peace. But now?" He shakes his head, disappointment clear in his eyes. "Sharon's actions have blurred those lines, and it's every person for themselves."

I lean in to absorb his words. My elbows are on my knees, and my fingers are intertwined. "Can you give me an example?"

"Take the community center," he says, his hands clasped tightly together. "It used to be neutral ground, a safe space for everyone. Now, however, it's a battleground for territorial disputes because Sharon decided it was a convenient place to conduct her business."

I remember the center well, a place where I'd spent countless afternoons as a kid. The thought of it becoming corrupted is a bitter pill to swallow.

"And the locally owned businesses," Father McCarry continues, "they're being squeezed for protection money more aggressively than ever. It's not just about survival anymore—it's about profit at the expense of our own people. Shopkeepers I've known for years are closing down, Maura. It's heartbreaking."

His words paint a bleak picture that resonates with the whispers I've heard and the changes I've seen with my own eyes. "It's like she's tearing the fabric of the neighborhood apart," I say, the realization hitting me hard.

"Exactly," he agrees, his gaze meeting mine. "And it's not just the physical changes, either. It's the loss of a sense of community, of belonging. People are afraid, Maura. They are afraid to speak out, afraid of what might happen if they do. Sharon's reign has introduced a level of fear we've never seen before."

"Sharon's gotta step down. She's causing too much chaos. But what can I do about it? I feel so helpless, and I don't know where to begin." It's like I'm throwing a lifeline out, hoping for some genius idea to come back and slap me in the head.

Father McCarry gives me a look, one that suggests he's got a trick up his sleeve. "Do you ever think about taking another peek at your dad's will, Maura? Perhaps there's something in there that was overlooked."

The thought stops me cold. "But Sharon had her lawyer go over it," I tell him, feeling a bit of a jolt. "I didn't even think to question it. I guess I was too wrapped up in my own grief."

Suddenly, his idea doesn't just feel like a shot in the dark but more like a beacon lighting my way out that I otherwise hadn't noticed. "You think Dad's will might have something in it that could put a stop to her?"

"Definitely worth a look," he says encouragingly. "Your dad's words might just be the ace we need."

Thinking about digging back into the will, something I let Sharon's lawyer paint any which way he wanted, doesn't seem so scary now. It feels like a chance to gain back some control and maybe save what's left of this mess.

"I'm going to read it word for word myself, then get someone who actually knows what they're doing to check it out," I state confidently, feeling a new resolve forming within.

"That's the spirit," Father McCarry says with a smile, sounding like he's already halfway to celebrating. "If you find anything in there, even the smallest little detail that Sharon missed, we might be able to turn this whole ship around."

And just like that, a plan is hatched. Not just any plan, but one that feels solid, like something I can actually accomplish, start to finish. It's not just about knocking Sharon down a peg; it's about doing right by my dad's memory and fixing the mess that's been made.

Father McCarry suddenly gets a look on his face like he's just hit the jackpot and starts digging around in his desk as if looking for treasure. He pulls out a business card and hands it over like it's the golden ticket to the Chocolate Factory. "Take this," he says in all seriousness. "The guy's a legal wizard, and he's been with the church forever. I'd trust him with my life."

"Frank Dreschel," I say out loud as I read the card, locking the name in my brain. "Thanks a million, Father. This could be the game-changer that we need."

He gives me a smile that makes me feel like everything's going to be okay. "Anytime, Maura. And hey," he adds, his eyes lighting up, "you know you've always got a place here. Whether you're looking for some peace, a bit of quiet, or just a place to gather your thoughts. Never forget you're welcome at any time, day or night."

His words hit me right in the belly, taking me back to a time when things were simpler, when my belief was solid and unwavering. "I won't forget," I tell him, truly meaning it.

After a warm hug goodbye, I exit Father McCarry's office and take a moment to stand in the church. The candlelight and the saintly faces in the stained glass give me a mix of comfort and nostalgia. It's a quick breath of peace before diving back into the whirlwind that's my life right now.

Walking out of St. Brigid's with Frank Dreschel's card in my grip, I've got a new spark of hope. There are still a lot of unknowns and risks, but for the first time in what seems like forever, I don't feel like I'm in it alone. Father McCarry's belief in me, his subtle push toward returning to the church, is not only a nice gesture but a lifeline, a reminder of the strength rooted deep within me thanks to where I come from and the community that raised me.

The fight to restore my family's name to the community's good graces and shield everyone from Sharon's fallout is just getting started. But with new friends in my corner and a fresh burst of determination, I'm more than ready to take on whatever's coming.

I step outside; the air's crisp bite makes me feel more alive and even more ready to tackle the mess ahead. Frank Dreschel's card is still in my grasp, and before I even realize it, I'm dialing the number with urgency.

The secretary's surprise is palpable through the phone when I tell her who I am. "Yes, that's me," I say, trying to sound more confident than I feel.

Before I know it, Frank's on the line, sounding like the kind of guy who means business. After I lay it all out for him—the will, Sharon's shady dealings, our family's tainted reputation in the community—he's all in. "Let's meet tomorrow," he says, and I can almost hear the gears turning in his head. "Give me a bit of time to get everything ready."

Hanging up, I feel a little flame of hope flickering inside me. Knowing Frank's on board, taking on Sharon doesn't feel so impossible anymore. It's like I've been handed a key, and I'm about to unlock a whole heap of secrets.

A grin breaks out on my face as I pocket my phone. Thinking about the meeting with Frank, about actually being able to do something to cut through the web that Sharon has spun, has me feeling all kinds of determined.

I had asked the Uber driver to wait for me, and as I head to where the car is parked, my steps are full of purpose and my mind is racing with plans. It is like I've got a map in my head, and I'm about to start the treasure hunt.

Suddenly, out of nowhere, a car pulls up and the driver quickly rolls down the window, explaining that he will be my new Uber driver and that my original driver had an emergency. I start to reach for the car door, but the driver jumps out before I can, opening the door for me. I start to climb inside before I notice that the driver is running away.

Then, my world explodes into chaos as a thunderous roar shatters the quiet neighborhood, and a blinding flash of light envelops me.

And then there's nothing but black.

CHAPTER 17

MAURA

The world slowly stops spinning on its axis, like someone's gradually turning down the speed on a merry-go-round. My ears are ringing, blocking out any other sound. When things finally come into focus, I'm staring at what looks like a scene from an action movie gone wrong.

Debris is everywhere, and the car is on fire. People are rushing over, a mix of bravery and concern on their faces. "Are you okay?" they shout at me over the noise. I manage a weak nod, but I'm freaking out on the inside, wondering if anyone else was injured in the blast.

"Was anyone else hurt?" The question comes out weakly.

"No, just you," someone says, and I'm caught between feeling relieved and utterly alone. Relief edges out, but it's a bittersweet win.

The ambulance siren cuts through the haze, growing louder as it nears, a beacon of hope in a sea of chaos. There I am, smack in the middle of it all. So much for my incognito trip away from the mansion.

As the paramedics hustle over, I can't help but think about how this whole mess is a giant, flashing sign that I'm onto something big. Someone went to a lot of trouble to scare me or even try and take me out of the picture for good.

As the EMTs load me onto the stretcher, my brain shifts into high gear. Sharon, the will, the family secrets—they're all clues in this twisted mystery I'm involved in. And if someone's desperate enough to pull a stunt like this to keep me from digging into it, then I must be getting close to something they don't want to be found.

This isn't a game anymore. As the ambulance doors close, hiding the fiery wreck from view, I swear to myself that whoever's behind the explosion is going to regret that they ever messed with a true Flanagan.

My surroundings are like a TV with bad reception, flickering in and out until everything snaps into sharp focus. I squint against the brightness of a hospital room, the quiet buzz of machines around me oddly comforting. It's now morning, and outside the window, Chicago goes on about its day, oblivious to the chaos going on in mine.

Twisting my head—a move I instantly regret—I catch sight of two hulks in suits loitering by my door. Bodyguards.

Just as I'm mentally tallying up all the areas where I hurt, the door swings open and in walks a woman with a chart in her hand.

"Morning," she says. I'm Dr. Susan Rivera. It looks like you've been playing a game of tag with consciousness, but it's good to have you fully back. How're you feeling?"

I lie there, trying to figure out how to answer her, seeing as I feel like I've gone a few rounds with a freight train. "I'm really sore, but otherwise okay. Is my husband here?"

Dr. Rivera pauses, choosing her words carefully. "Actually, before we get to that, there's something I need to talk to you about." That's all it takes for my brain to jump to DEFCON 1.

"Is something wrong?" I ask. The question sounds sharper than I intended.

Dr. Rivera tries to smooth things over with a smile, but my stomach's already doing somersaults. "It's not bad news, just... personal." Her attempt at calming me does little to dial down my anxiety.

"Tell me then," I push, my patience running thin. I need facts, not suspense. "Please," I add in a softer tone.

She takes a deep breath before dropping a bombshell. "Well, we did the standard bloodwork when you arrived, and it appears you're pregnant." She says it with a smile, trying to package it as good news.

It takes a second for her words to really hit home. *Pregnant*. Me? It's a lot to wrap my head around. It feels as if I've suddenly been handed a puzzle with half the pieces missing.

For a brief moment—the explosion, the constant danger, the multiple attempts on my life—all fade into the background.

This news reshuffles everything, putting this tiny new life at the center of my universe.

Dr. Rivera's expression softens as she notices my struggle to grasp the reality of her news. "I wanted to tell you first, alone, so that you can figure out how you want to tell your husband," she explains, her voice gentle, understanding.

"Thank you," I manage, my mind racing with thoughts of the future, of Luk and me, of the unexpected life growing inside me. The gratitude I feel for her sensitivity is genuine, even if it's overshadowed by my distant response due to the whirlwind of emotions I'm experiencing.

Our conversation is cut short by the sight of Luk approaching the room. His presence is like a storm rolling in, his eyes dark with an intensity that speaks volumes. He pushes open the door, the very air seeming to shift around him.

Dr. Rivera stands her ground, professionalism personified. "Mr. Ivanov, I know you're concerned, but Maura's not yet ready for visitors," she asserts, trying to buffer the tension.

Luk's gaze is unwavering, his voice low and demanding. "I need to see my wife," he firmly states, leaving no room for argument.

Dr. Rivera looks to me for guidance, her expression asking the question her lips do not. The sight of Luk at that moment—so fiercely protective, so unmistakably present—I feel a wave of relief wash over me. "It's fine," I say, my voice sounding stronger than I feel. "He can stay."

As I look at my husband, his presence steadies me. His eyes find mine, and I can see the battle raging behind his gaze—so many conflicting emotions fighting to express themselves.

I can see what he's feeling as he gets closer: pissed off, confused, scared, relieved. It's all right there on his face. And a realization hits me hard—no matter how crazy things get, there's no one else I want standing beside me.

Luk gently sits down on the edge of my bed. "I ought to be mad at you for going rogue," he starts, and I can hear the emotion in his voice. "And I am. But mostly, I'm just damn glad you're still here." He grabs my hand, and just like that, I'm anchored. He's looking at me like he's trying to read my mind. "What has the doctor told you?" he asks, searching my eyes for immediate answers. I look to Dr. Rivera still standing at the foot of my bed. I give her a look that I hope she can read before she speaks.

"Your wife suffered a minor concussion and mild smoke inhalation, along with plenty of bruises and contusions, Mr. Ivanov. She'll need lots of fluids and plenty of rest, but I'm comfortable releasing her if you can assure me that she'll get what she needs." She returns a look that tells me she understood that I wasn't ready to reveal the pregnancy just yet.

"Trust me, Doctor. I will be wait on my wife hand and foot for as long as she needs," Luk replies. I've already hired a private, in-home nurse to tend to her while she recovers."

Hearing that, I'm torn. I want to get out of the hospital as quickly as possible, yet I'm dreading stepping back into our world—a world where it seems like we're always looking over our shoulders. But I'm starting to feel like Luk and I are a true team, and that maybe we can handle this—together.

CHAPTER 18

LUK

My gaze is locked on Maura, watching her every expression as she's assisted into a wheelchair. The sight ignites a fury in me, a reminder of her vulnerability and of the danger that came so close to snatching her away from me yet again. As I follow the nurse pushing Maura toward the staff's private elevators, my mind races with violent thoughts of retribution against whoever continues to target her.

We reach the ground floor and are escorted toward an exit that leads into the parking garage, where my driver is waiting. She's carefully settled into the back of our bulletproof SUV, a precaution that now feels more like a necessity. Once she's secure, I slide in next to her, so many unspoken words swirling inside my head. But my barely contained rage prevents me from speaking as I clench and unclench my fists.

As the car pulls out of the parking garage and away from the hospital grounds, I can't help but replay the day's events in my head, each moment fueling my anger further. "They're going to pay for this," I mutter under my breath, the vow slipping out like a dark promise.

Maura turns to me, her eyebrows drawn together in worry. "Luk," she starts, her voice steady despite everything she's been through, "I know you're angry, but—"

"But nothing," I cut in; the words are sharp, a reflection of the turmoil churning inside me. "They almost took you from me—again. I can't... I *won't* let that go."

The car weaves through Chicago's busy streets, but the outside world might as well be miles away for all the attention I give it. My focus is on Maura, on the promise I need to make to her. "I'm going to find out who's behind this," I declare, meeting her eyes, needing her to see the depth and sincerity of my words. "And when I do, they, and anyone else involved, will wish they'd never crossed us."

She reaches for my hand, her grip firm. "Luk, I'm scared, but knowing you're here, that you're fighting for us... it gives me strength, makes me feel safer," she admits, her voice laced with a bravery that fills me with awe.

My gaze frequently shifts to the windows, eyes scanning for any sign of danger. The need to protect Maura, to ensure no harm comes her way ever again, has my senses on high alert.

I steal glances at her every so often, noticing the way she appears lost in thought as if she's wrestling with something deep within. It's clear she's holding something back from me, some piece of information or concern she's not ready to share yet. The urge to know what it is, to help shoulder whatever burden she's carrying, is strong, but I respect her need to come to terms with things in her own time.

The SUV finally pulls up to our home, allowing a brief sense of relief. The mansion stands like a bastion against the threats of the world outside, its walls providing a protective promise of safety and security.

Unbeknownst to Maura, intense plans to ramp up security were put into place moments after the attack on her in her bedroom. During Maura's short hospital stay, those plans were finalized—more guards, enhanced video surveillance, including more security cameras around the mansion and the grounds, and motion sensors inconspicuously placed in multiple locations inside and out. I feel as if a small semblance of control has returned, though the fact that she was able to leave undetected still does not sit well with me.

I turn to Maura, noting the tension in her posture. "Hey, you're home," I say softly, offering her a small, reassuring smile. "You're safe here. We can discuss the details later but I've increased the level of security significantly. No one will ever breach these walls again without being detected."

The driver opens my door, and I step out, rounding the vehicle to assist my wife. I tenderly help her, careful not to grasp her too firmly. I wrap my arm around her waist as we step up the stairs leading to the front doors. "Where do you want to go first?" I ask Maura as we step inside, doing my best to keep the anger at bay, replacing it instead with a concern that's become all too familiar recently.

"The library," she decides without a moment's hesitation, her voice carrying that unmistakable note of determination. I need to feel a sense of normalcy, doing something other than lying in bed feeling like an invalid, which I am not," she quickly adds. Her words, laced with a stubbornness that's both infuriating and endearing, make me smile.

As she settles into one of the chairs, I head over to the grand fireplace and strike a match to light a fire. Outside, rain begins to patter against the windows, and a soft, rhythmic sound fills the room.

The fire crackles to life, casting a warm glow over the room, and a comfortable silence envelops us. At that moment, with the storm outside and the warmth of the fire battling the chill, I know it's time to address the new reality of our lives.

I take a seat opposite her, the seriousness of the moment pressing down on me. "Maura," I begin, my voice steady, "there are going to be some new rules around the house. All are for your safety. You're not going out again without security, and the fact that you were able to leave without anyone knowing was a one-time anomaly," I state firmly.

Maura's frustration is immediate. "I feel trapped here. I need some semblance of freedom," she counters, her tone brimming with the willpower I've come to admire so deeply.

My heart twists at her plea, torn between the instinct to protect and the desire to grant her the freedom she craves. "I get it, I do. But as long as there continues to be attempts made on your life, it's not safe," I reply, trying to bridge the gap between my fears and her needs. "Surely, you can understand that."

She shakes her head, her spirit unyielding. "I do understand that, but I can't live in constant fear either, Luk. I need—"

I cut her off, not out of annoyance, but out of an overwhelming fear of losing her, of the need to get through to her. "I will not, cannot, let you just walk into danger, Maura," My voice comes out louder than I intended, echoing off the library walls. "This is not a game; it's about keeping you alive. I can't do that if you're not here or if you're someplace unknown without the protection of your bodyguards."

Her eyes meet mine, and for a moment, we're locked in an unspoken battle of wills. "So are you saying I'm a prisoner now?" she challenges, the hurt clear in her voice.

"No, of course, you're not a prisoner; I never want you to feel that way in your own home. I just want you to feel protected. Please, let me sort this out. Once I know for certain you're no longer in danger, the restrictions will be lifted," I try to explain, my voice softening, imploring her to understand. "I'm doing this because the thought of something happening to you is unbearable."

The room falls silent, save for the crackling of the fire and the beats of raindrops on the windows, as we both grapple with the weight of the situation. "I just want you safe, and I can't stress that enough," I add more quietly now, hoping she can hear the sincerity in my words, the depth of my fear for her well-being.

Maura's expression softens, a silent acknowledgment of my concern over the impossible situation we're in. "I know. I know you're scared. I am, too," she admits, a truce of sorts.

I linger by her side, every instinct screaming at me to stay. I just want to wrap her in my arms and shield her from the world's cruelty, to allow someone else to handle this and prevent us from being apart. But with a heavy heart, I know what I must do.

"I have to take care of something," I tell her. Maura looks up at me, her eyes holding a world of understanding. She nods, a silent gesture of support that fuels the fire within me.

"I'm going to summon the Bratva," I declare. The words are a vow of war against those responsible for disrupting our peace and threatening my wife's life. "We're going to hold an emergency meeting, and I'm going to find out who's behind this. Whoever it is will be extinguished."

The promise hangs heavy in the room. I lean down, pressing a kiss to her forehead, displaying tenderness for a moment and proving my sincere feelings for her.

"I'll be back soon," I say, giving once last whispered promise. Then I turn and stride out of the library, my resolve tenfold as I'm hit with the realization of just how deep my feelings are for her.

We meet in the grand conference room, a space where strategies are established and where the might of the Bratva is rallied against our unseen enemies. The conference room is a testament to old-world Russian elegance—dark hardwoods and ornately carved moldings line the walls, which are filled with framed portraits of Bratva royalty. A large, imposing table sits in the center. The windows offer a sweeping view of the vast property that stretches toward the surrounding forest, which provides additional security courtesy of nature.

I pour myself a drink. The amber liquid is a temporary distraction as I wait for the others to arrive, but my thoughts invariably drift back to Maura and the secret that she's holding so close. I trust her to reveal it in her own time; pressuring her isn't my style.

Soon the room fills with the heart of the Bratva—Lev, Yuri, Elena, Grigori, and a cadre of trusted lieutenants, about ten in total. They file in, each wearing an expression of stoicism and readiness, prepared for whatever directives I have to give.

Once everyone's settled, I stand, my gaze sweeping over those gathered. "The gloves are off," I begin, my voice firm, resonant.

The room falls completely silent, the gravity of my words sinking in. This isn't just another skirmish, another dispute to be discussed and settled. This is a battle for my wife's safety and peace in our lives. And in this fight, I will not hold back or show any mercy.

"Prepare for war," I declare, letting the full weight of my command settle over the room. "We will find out who's behind these attacks on Maura, and we will make them pay."

For Maura, for the peace she deserves, I'll wage this war with every ounce of strength I possess. The Bratva stands united, and under my command, we'll face down any threat. This is our vow, our unbreakable promise of retribution.

CHAPTER 19

MAURA

It's too quiet in our room as I lie on the bed. Luk's side is empty, and I feel like he's been gone forever. I've been trying to write in my journal, but the notebook just sits there, staring back at me. I keep moving the pen around on the page, but no words issue forth. It's like my brain is too full of everything that has happened, and I'm unable to formulate any other thoughts.

We've only been married a little over two months, yet in that short time, I feel like we're the main characters in some crazy action movie. Finding out about my pregnancy should feel amazing, but with the threat of danger surrounding us, I can't help but feel scared. Really scared. I'm constantly wondering how Luk is going to react to the news. The timing of this baby couldn't be worse. Our enemies are lining up just as we're about to bring a new life into the world.

But regardless of how frightened I am, I can't sit around and do nothing. It's time to face things head-on. Sharon is at the center of many of my questions, and I am determined to pry the answers out of her.

I put the journal away. I've got to be smart and cautious. I have to dig into my family's secrets without causing a confrontation and without Sharon knowing.

I feel the clock ticking, and it's driving me crazy, like time is counting down to something big. I've got to make a move, and fast. I'm not going to let anyone threaten our little family. I get out of bed, feeling more determined than ever. I'm ready to take on whatever it is that's hiding in the dark for our sake and our baby's. It's time to find out the truth, no matter what.

The garden is alive with color, each flower basking in the morning sun. Lily is knee-deep in dirt and petals, looking every bit the garden goddess she is. Watching her work is like a hit of calm, something I am in desperate need of.

"Lily," I blurt out, my heart racing with the news I'd been carrying around. "I'm pregnant."

She freezes, hands in midair, dirt crumbling from her fingers, then whips around with a smile so big it nearly splits her face. "Oh, Maura! That's amazing! Perhaps it's not the best timing with all of this craziness, but still, amazing."

"Right?" I say, laughing, but it sounds more like a sigh. "I haven't even told Luk yet. How does one drop a bomb like this amongst all this mess?"

Lily stands and wipes her hands on her apron before coming over, her eyes shining with something fierce and protective. "Maura, that man cares deeply for you. This baby's going to be a beacon for you both. But yes, we need to make sure that everyone stays safe."

Her words are meant to lift me, and they do, but they also create a commotion inside me. I'm torn, standing on the edge of a cliff with my family's secrets on one side and my new, growing family on the other.

"I get that and thank you. It's just..." I trail off, my worries too big and tangled to put into words.

Lily steps closer, her warmth cutting through the morning chill. "Hey, whatever you need, I'm here. This place," she gestures around us, "is your fortress. And that little one?" She smiles gently as she points to my belly, "is going to be the most loved kid ever."

She wraps me in a hug, providing me with momentary comfort and a promise of support. But still, a battle wages within, hope and fear duking it out.

"Thanks, Lily," I manage to say, my voice thick. "I just need to figure all of this out. I have to figure out how to shield this baby from what's coming."

She squeezes my hand, her grip solid and sure. "You will. You're made of tough stuff. And you're not alone in this."

Lily's assurance is a spark in the dark, kindling that fire in me that had been smothered by fear and uncertainty. As we walk back toward the mansion, I know what I have to do. My family's secrets, Sharon's dealings... it's time to pull back the curtain, and I need Lily's help to do it.

That afternoon, we find a quiet nook in the house to hide in, a secluded corner that feels miles away from the chaos.

Daylight streams through the windows, casting patterns on the floor, a reminder that life, with all its complexities, still moves forward.

"Lily," I tell her in a whisper, "I need to dig into my step-mother's activities. There's something she's not telling me, something that could be the key to all this madness."

Lily's eyebrows shoot up, but she nods, her usual warmth tempered with seriousness. "You think she's involved in the attempts on your life?"

"I honestly don't know," I admit, feeling the weight of my suspicions. But I can't shake the feeling that she knows more than she's letting on. Luk's way of handling things is direct and powerful, but this needs a subtler touch. I don't want to start an all-out war without knowing what we're walking into."

Lily leans in, her eyes sharp. "How can I help? You know I'm with you every step of the way."

A smile tugs at the corners of my mouth. I am so grateful for her unwavering support. "First, I need to get my hands on any financial records and communications, including emails and phone calls, anything that might give us a clue to what she's been up to. I'm thinking of starting with the business dealings. There have to be traces somewhere."

"Smart," Lily nods, her mind already ticking over the possi-bilities. "I can start poking around—discreetly, of course. I'll bet there are people in the family who aren't as loyal to Sharon as she thinks they are. That could be a way in."

"And," I continue, the plan crystallizing with each word, "we need to do this without alerting Luk. At least not yet.

He'd go in, guns blazing, and that's the last thing we need right now."

Lily's agreement is immediate. "Understood. We'll keep it quiet, just between the two of us. Luk's got enough on his plate, and the last thing he needs is to worry about internal family drama."

As we map out our strategy, I can't help but feel both excitement and dread. The path ahead is fraught with danger, but the need to protect my family, to protect the little life growing inside me, outweighs any fear.

"Thanks, Lil," I say, feeling a surge of affection for the woman who's become more than just staff, more than just a friend. She's become like family to me. "I don't know what I'd do without you."

She squeezes my hand, a gesture of solidarity. "You'd do just fine. But the good news is you don't have to. We're in this together."

CHAPTER 20

LUK

Walking through Bridgeport feels like stepping into another world that's far removed from the high-stakes drama of our lives. The neighborhood's got an old-school, lived-in vibe, with brick houses standing shoulder to shoulder like aging soldiers. There's a sense of community here that's strong and obvious, even to someone like me, who's more accustomed to the cutthroat dynamics of the Bratva.

Lev breaks the silence, his voice cutting through the city's hum. "You know, brother, I've noticed something different about you lately."

I shoot him a glare, the kind that would send most men scurrying. "Don't start, Lev. We're not here to talk about my personal life."

But Lev just smirks, undeterred by my warning. "Come on. It's written all over your face. You're head over heels for her. When's the last time you looked at anyone the way you look at Maura?"

I grumble, knowing that he's not entirely wrong. "It's not like that. We're just... it's complicated, all right?"

Lev laughs, a sound that's both annoying and somehow comforting. It's a brother thing, I suppose. "Complicated," he says. "Luk, everything's complicated when it comes to love. But in a good way. You're in it, deep. Looks good on you."

I shake my head, trying to steer the conversation away from dangerous waters. "Focus, Lev. We're here for a reason. Maura's safety is our top priority."

He nods, but I can tell he's not ready to let it go. "All right. But just remember, brother, love makes us stronger, not weaker. Maura's making you a better man."

I don't have a comeback for that, mainly because part of me knows he's right. Maura has changed me in ways I'm still trying to understand myself. But right now, there are bigger issues at hand.

"We'll talk about this later," I finally concede, knowing full well that later means never if I can help it. "Right now, we need to figure out who it is that's after her and why."

Lev nods, a sign that he's willing to drop the subject for now. "Agreed, but so that you know, we're all rooting for you two. Maura's one of us now."

We step into O'Malley's, a corner tavern that wears its Irish heritage like a badge of honor. The dark wood paneling, stained glass windows depicting Celtic knots, and the ever-present aroma of stout and whiskey create an inviting and unmistakably Irish ambiance. A few heads turn as we make our entrance. We're recognized either by reputation or by the fact that we stand out like sore thumbs.

Without missing a beat, we slide into a booth, and I signal the bartender for a round of Guinness. The foam-topped dark stouts arrive quickly. I take a moment to survey the room, noting the tattoos adorning the arms of several patrons—a few of them Irish mob insignias. It's clear we've found the hangout of the neighborhood's underworld.

The bartender, a stocky man with a face as weathered as the bar he tends, approaches our booth with a cautious curiosity. "What can I do for you, gentlemen?" he asks with a thick brogue—no doubt a first-generation immigrant like myself. The look he gives me makes it clear he knows exactly who I am.

I lean forward; my tone is casual yet commanding. "We're looking for information. There's been some trouble, and we believe it's connected to someone from around here."

The bartender's eyes narrow slightly as he raises his chin, suspicion and recognition flashing through them. "Trouble, aye? We've got no shortage of that around here. But I'm not sure how much help I can be to you lads."

Lev chimes in, his voice smooth and reassuring. "We're not here to cause problems. We just need to understand what's going on and why."

I nod, adding, "It concerns the safety of someone very close to us. We think there's a connection here. Any information you have could be crucial and will be very much appreciated."

The bartender pauses, considering our words. Then, with a resigned sigh, he sits down opposite us. "All right, I'll hear you out. But I can't promise anything. This place, these people, we look out for our own, just as I suspect your kind does."

I acknowledge his stance with a nod. "Understood. And we respect that. But believe me when I say the safety of my wife is non-negotiable. We will seek out the information we need, one way or another."

"And what is it exactly that you're looking to find out?" he asks.

"Sharon Flanagan. Or Sharon Halsey, as she was known before her marriage. I want to know everything you know about her."

I notice a flicker of recognition in his eyes—a spark that tells me we're about to wade into dangerous waters. "Sharon, aye?" he muses, leaning closer as if the walls themselves might be eavesdropping. "Now, that's a name I haven't heard in a good while around these parts."

Lev and I exchange a look, both of us sensing the shift in the air. "You know, I don't believe that one bit."

The bartender hesitates, glancing around the dimly lit pub as if reassessing the wisdom of speaking freely. "Look, as I said before, I don't want any trouble," he says, his voice lowering. "But if you're going to be asking about Sharon, you should know this place has a history with her."

Lev shifts his posture, his demeanor commanding. "We're not here to stir up the past for no good reason. Trust me when I say there is a purpose behind every move we make and every question we ask."

Taking a deep breath, the bartender begins to unravel the tale. "This pub," he begins, "was started by my father. And from what I've heard, it was like a second home to Sharon when she was a teenager. She skipped more classes than she attended, always trying to prove she wasn't your average Catholic schoolgirl. She was ambitious, even back then. She made friends with some of the local lads who had connected families, families like the ones Rory Murphy comes from."

I absorb his words, each piece adding depth to the puzzle of Sharon's past. "Rory," I echo, the name carrying more weight now. "So, this is where she pulled him into her orbit?"

"That's right," the bartender confirms. Rory was just another kid from the neighborhood in those days. But Sharon had plans—always did. She brought him into the fold, you could say. She helped him rise up the ranks until he became her right-hand man, her bodyguard. That boy would do anything for her."

The pieces begin to click into place, a clearer image of Sharon's manipulation and immoral ambition emerging from the bartender's account. Her influence, it seems, started much earlier than anyone realized, sowing seeds that would grow into the tangled web we're now trying to unravel.

"Thank you," I say to the bartender, my words genuine. "It's clear Sharon's been playing the long game."

The bartender nods. "I know you lads are more than capable of handling yourselves but be careful; Sharon's got a reach and a reputation around here. Not all of it is good."

Lev and I listen intently, absorbing every detail. "There's always been talk," the bartender says with a hint of disdain, "about Sharon and Rory being more than just employer and bodyguard if you catch my drift. It's business; Rory was just a lad."

I nod, the implications clear. "And after she married Mickey Flanagan?" I press, wanting to understand the full scope of her betrayals.

The bartender shrugs. It's a gesture that conveys the open secret of their relationship. "No one could prove anything, but let's just say Rory's been more than just a shadow to Sharon. He's her enforcer, her confidant, and probably more."

Lev leans back, his expression darkening at the thought. "And what of her leadership? How's she managing the Flanagan family?" he asks, his interest piqued by the bartender's earlier insinuations of incompetence.

The bartender lets out a short, humorless laugh. "Leadership? If you want to call it that. Sharon's got pride to spare but not the sense to back it up. She's been trying to fill her father's shoes and now Mickey's, but she's stumbling. Her attempts to keep the Flanagan name afloat are pathetic, frankly. She's squandering what's left of her father's legacy, and Mickey's along with it."

I glance at Lev, both of us recognizing the gravity of the bartender's words. Sharon's actions, driven by pride and a lack of competence, have put at risk not just the Flanagan legacy but also Maura and our family. But to what end?

"Any specific machinations we should be aware of?" I ask, my tone hardening. "Anything that could explain the attempts on my wife's life?"

The bartender leans in again, his voice dropping to a whisper. "Yeah, there's been some buzz about that. It's an awful thing. The word is Sharon's desperate. She's been making risky moves, trying to shore up her position, borrowing from Peter to pay Paul. There's talk of debts—big ones—owed to some dangerous people. Apparently, she's used up her inheritance from Mick, and now she's playing a dangerous game that she's not equipped to win."

More pieces of the puzzle fall into place, forming a clearer picture of Sharon's desperation and the lengths she's willing to go to maintain a semblance of power.

As the bartender concludes his tale, Lev and I share a glance, our minds racing with the implications of his words. "Thanks again for the information and for taking the time to speak with us," I say, offering a nod of appreciation. You've given us a lot to think about."

The weight of Maura's safety hangs heavy between us, coloring every word as we watch the bartender make his way back across the pub.

Lev breaks the silence, his tone serious: "Luk, we've got to find out how deep Sharon's involvement is in all of this. We may need to warn Maura."

I nod, thinking the same thing. "Absolutely. But we're going to be smart about this, Lev. We need to approach it in the right way. No diving headfirst without a solid plan."

Understanding passes between us, a silent vow that we'll do everything in our power to keep Maura out of harm's way. Whatever it takes.

I sit back and scan the room, eyeing the pub's patrons for any sign of hidden threats or alliances.

My gaze lands on a group photo hanging on the wall, a momentary distraction before my thoughts realign. "All right. We lay low but pass this information along to security and tell them to up their surveillance without making Maura suspect anything's amiss. It's about her feeling safe, not trapped."

We talk strategy and how to tighten the security net around Maura without her feeling the squeeze. It's a fine line to walk, motivated by the deep-seated need to protect the woman I have come to love without suffocating her spirit. I've finally admitted to myself the depth of my feelings for her, and that admittance has only bolstered my protective instincts.

Rising to leave, my mind is on Maura, picturing her laugh and the way her eyes light up in amusement. The thought of her safety, her happiness, her everything propels me forward, ready to face whatever comes our way. Lev's steady support and our brotherly bond feel like a solid anchor as we head out into the evening, the city's distant noises a backdrop to our shared purpose.

"Whatever it takes," I reaffirm aloud, the words echoing in the cool night air.

CHAPTER 21

MAURA

The sunlight sneaks in through the boutique's huge windows, throwing a cozy glow over the fancy clothes within. Elena and I are strolling through the place, arms linked, pretending everything's normal for a minute. It'd taken some serious convincing for Luk to let me out of the house, and only on the condition that a pair of hulking bodyguards accompany Elena and me.

But even with our giggles and the sound of hangers clicking, there's still a feeling hovering over me like a shadow, one that's been tailing me ever since I became Maura Ivanova.

Elena doesn't know that I'm using part of our outing to sneak off to see Frank, the lawyer. I feel guilty for not looping her in, but it's something I must do alone.

"He's just worried that you could be hurt again," Elena says. Her voice cuts into my thoughts, her tone breezy in an attempt to lighten the mood. "Luk's not trying to be controlling. He's genuinely concerned about you."

I run my fingers over a silky baby blue dress. It feels as if it's made of water. "Yes, I know he's not trying to be a dictator or anything like that," I say, the words tasting sour. "I just hate feeling caged in, even if the cage is a really nice one."

Elena grabs a satin scarf, wraps it around her neck, and looks at me past her reflection in a mirror. "The more he cares, the more he's going to worry, and the more he worries, the tighter he's going to hold on."

There's a beat where her words truly sink in. I've seen the way Luk looks at me, all tender and gentle-like, a total 180 from the tough guy he shows the rest of the world. "I only wish he could understand that I need a bit of space, a chance to breathe," I half-whisper, talking to myself more than Elena.

Elena faces me; her expression is serious. "He understands more than you think. But every time you head out that door, it's like his world stops. Don't you see? It's not about keeping you on a leash. It's about something happening to you, Maura. It's a fear that he can't overcome."

That's when it hits me how deep Luk's affection reaches, an affection that would start wars or burn down cities just to keep me safe. I can see how scared he is, and I understand now how far he'd go to protect me.

"We're going to figure this out," Elena says, her voice gentle and sure. "Together, we'll show him you can be both safe and free."

Her words help smooth over the rough spots in my heart. As we keep shopping, letting the laughter creep back in, I start to feel a bit of hope. Maybe she's right; maybe there is a way to balance safety and freedom. Maybe Luk and I can walk this tricky path side by side, finding our way back to each other along the way.

In a heartbeat, Elena's vibe shifts from sisterly advice-giver to chief fun coordinator. "You know what? Let's take a breather from this shopping marathon. I'm starving, and I bet you are, too," she declares, her eyes looking for an escape route from the endless sea of luxury goods.

Grateful for the distraction, I nod eagerly. "Food sounds amazing right now."

We weave our way out of the boutique, laughter and light banter leading us down the Miracle Mile. The street is buzzing with energy, a symphony of honking cars, chattering pedestrians, and the distant hum of music. It feels good to be out here, away from the stuffiness of high-end shops, breathing in the city's vibrant, spirited life.

Elena points ahead, her excitement tangible. "There! That place has the cutest little outdoor seating."

We snag a table outside, the mild breeze a pleasant companion to our meal. As we peruse the menu, I can't help but feel a wave of gratitude for Elena's presence. She's a breath of fresh air, pulling me out of the spiral of worry and anxiety that's become my norm. I'm so comfortable and having so much fun that I can almost ignore the huge, suited bodyguards posted nearby. Almost.

Elena's enthusiasm for the menu manages to distract me for a moment. "The quiche here is legendary," she insists, her eyes sparkling with the kind of excitement usually reserved for major life events, and I can't help but smile. I nod, trying to muster the same level of enthusiasm while my brain is doing mental gymnastics, planning my escape to see Frank Dreschel. I need to play this just right.

The moment I start to relax, thinking I might actually pull it off, my stomach decides to betray me. It's like a sudden squall at sea—calm one minute, turbulent the next. I clamp my mouth shut, willing the nausea to pass.

Elena's sharp, and nothing gets past her. My feeble attempt at covering the nausea is a complete failure. "Are you all right?" she asks, searching my face, her expression one of legitimate concern.

I force a laugh, hoping it sounds more convincing than it feels. "Absolutely," I lie through my teeth. "I guess my stomach didn't get the memo about today's caffeine limit." It's a flimsy excuse, but it's all I've got, and seeing as we stopped for coffee before shopping, I hoped it would suffice.

Without missing a beat, Elena switches into full-on protective mode. "Okay, that's it. We're going for the ginger tea. And how about a salad? Something light and simple," she decides, signaling the waiter. I can't help but feel a twinge of guilt for deceiving her, even if it's for a good cause. "Ginger tea sounds perfect," I concede, grateful for the change of subject and the reprieve it offers from the unease churning in my belly.

But as we enjoy our drinks, part of me is still plotting, still scheming. I need to see Frank Dreschel delve into the mystery of my father's will without tipping off Luk or anyone else to my plans. The thought of sneaking around behind Elena's back gnaws at me, but I remind myself it's for the greater good.

Lunch continues with an easy flow, but I feel an underlying tension, like Elena's playing detective, piecing together clues I didn't even know I was dropping. Her next move catches me off guard, her eyes twinkling with mischief. "How about we celebrate your grand day out with some bubbly?" she suggests, her tone casual but her gaze sharp.

My stomach tenses. "Actually, I think I'll pass on the champagne," I say, hoping my voice doesn't betray the panic setting in.

Elena leans back, a knowing smile spreading across her face. "A-ha!" she exclaims, her expression one of triumph and warmth. My gut does a nosedive. Somehow, without me saying a word, Elena's figured it out. The realization that I'm not as slick as I thought sends a jolt of anxiety through me. How did she know? What gave me away? My mind races through our conversation, trying to pinpoint the moment my secret slipped through the cracks.

But as I sit there, frozen in place, Elena's reaction is far from what I expected. There's no judgment, no interrogation. Instead, there's a feeling of understanding, of sisterhood.

"Go on," she says with a smile. "Admit it."

A heavy moment hangs between us until, at last, I let out a resigned sigh, the secret already out of the bag anyway. "Okay, yes, I'm pregnant," I confess, feeling both relief and apprehension at admitting it.

Elena's response is immediate and exuberant, a burst of joy that fills the space around us. "I knew it!" she exclaims, her excitement a living thing. "This is amazing, Maura!"

Her happiness is infectious, and despite the whirlwind of emotions I'm feeling, I can't help but crack a smile.

Without missing a beat, Elena flags down the waiter, ordering a bottle of sparkling water for me and a glass of champagne for herself. Once the drinks arrive, she raises her glass and, with a genuine smile that's equal parts happy and excited, says, "To new beginnings."

After we clink glasses, I ask, "How did you guess?"

Elena's grin widens, and she nods, a hint of mischief in her eyes. "Yes. I might have taken a peek at your hospital files after the accident," she admits, her tone casual but apologetic.

My jaw drops, a mix of shock and amusement at her audacity. "You hacked into my medical records?" I ask, incredulous yet not surprised to hear that she went to such lengths.

Elena shrugs, and I shake my head, laughter bubbling up despite the initial shock. "Well, I guess I can't be too mad. You'd find out sooner or later," I concede, raising my glass of sparkling water in a mock salute. "You are, after all, the baby's auntie."

As I sit across from Elena, my heart does somersaults. It feels like madness to drop the baby bomb on Luk now when our lives are more tangled than a season of some convoluted reality show.

Elena, picking at her salad, looks up with those knowing eyes. "So, when are you planning to tell him?"

I sigh, pushing my food around my own plate. "Elena, how can I? With everything that's going on right now, it just doesn't seem fair to pile this on him, too."

She laughs, a light, easy sound that somehow makes it feel less like a crisis. "Maura, Luk's tough. Sure, he's got that whole brooding, Bratva boss thing down, but this? This will make him the happiest man alive."

"But the threats, the attacks..." I try to argue, but she waves me off.

"Maura, love," she leans in, her tone earnest. Luk's been through worse. This, you, us, is what he's protecting. What's one more reason to keep fighting, especially one of such great importance?"

I chew on my lip, considering. "I just... I need some time, Elena, to figure out how to tell him."

She nods in understanding. "Okay, I get it, but don't wait too long. Secrets have a way of making themselves known, and usually at the worst possible times."

I smile, grateful for her support. "Thanks, Elena. I don't know what I'd do without you."

She grins, raising her glass. "Probably get into less trouble. But where's the fun in that?"

Our laughter fills the space between us, easing the tension. For a moment, everything feels surprisingly normal.

The last crumbs of our indulgent lunch disappear, and Elena makes a suggestion. "How about we hit a few more stores before we head back? I heard there's a sale at Saks, and I want to check it out."

I glance at my watch, seeing that the time for my appointment is near. "Yes, that sounds great," I reply, the words slipping out before I can think better of them. The thought of diving back into the world of retail therapy is tempting, a distraction I'm eager to lose myself in, even if just for a little while longer.

We pay the bill and head out. But as we approach the gleaming entrance of the department store, a knot forms in my stomach. I sneak another glance at my watch and realize with a jolt that my window of opportunity is closing fast. If I'm going to make my appointment with Frank, I need to leave immediately.

Elena and I step into Saks, and I can't help but feel a major twinge of guilt for what I'm about to do. She's chatting away, excited about some exclusive collection that just arrived, but my mind is focused on something else entirely.

"We could split up and cover more ground," Elena suggests, eyeing the sprawling floors. "We might be able to accomplish more that way."

I nod, disbelieving the opportunity I've just been given. "Great idea. Can I meet you back here in an hour?"

"Deal. Don't get lost," she winks, heading toward the escalator. "And don't try to ditch your bodyguard either!" she adds over her shoulder.

I have one hour. The office is ten minutes away. I might be able to finish the meeting with Frank and get back here before she suspects anything.

As soon as she's out of sight, I tell the guard that remains with me that I need to use the restroom. He nods and stands out front with his back to the door. Thankfully, there is a small commotion as two women start to argue over one remaining sweater on a rack, and I am able to slip away without him noticing.

Ducking through a side door marked 'Employees Only,' I slip into the back corridors of the store, my steps quick and quiet.

Emerging on the opposite side, I glance back to make sure I'm not being followed before hailing a cab. "Downtown, and step on it," I tell the driver, sinking low into the seat as we pull away.

CHAPTER 22

MAURA

As the city blurs past, I feel guilty for betraying Elena. She's been nothing but supportive, and here I am, ditching her, all to play Nancy Drew with my family's dark legacy. But this isn't about Elena; it's about Luk, our baby, and securing a future free from the dangers of my family's past.

My conscience berates me as I scroll through the unread messages piling up on my phone. Finally, I cave and read through Elena's texts. They range from mildly concerned to full-blown panic mode to anger.

Where are you?

Are you okay?

If you haven't been kidnapped, I'm going to kick your ass.

So much for sneaking back.

I switch off my phone, a lump forming in my throat. Going dark feels like stepping off a cliff, but I can't take the risk that Luk or his Bratva buddies can track me. Besides, I only need an hour or so.

The cab pulls up in front of a towering skyscraper, all glass and cold, hard steel. It's the kind of place that screams power and money, and not necessarily in that order. I step out, squaring my shoulders as I face the imposing building.

The lobby is all sleek lines and hushed tones, the kind of quiet that makes my footsteps sound like gunshots. I make a beeline for the elevators, hitting the button for Mr. Dreschel's floor with more force than necessary. The ride up is a slow climb to Judgment Day, my stomach flip-flopping like a fish out of water.

The attorney's office looks just like I remember it, all plush carpeting and elegant upholstery. The air is thick with a seriousness that makes my heart sink a little lower with each step. Something's off. The receptionist looks like she's carrying the weight of the world on her shoulders.

"Hi, I'm Maura Flanagan. I have an appointment with Mr. Dreschel," I announce with a smile, trying to inject a bit of enthusiasm into the somber atmosphere.

The receptionist meets my gaze, and I catch a glimpse of genuine worry flickering in her eyes. It's a look that says whatever she's about to tell me isn't good. She hesitates, her voice softening, "Ms. Flanagan, I'm so sorry. I meant to call you..."

A pause hangs between us, heavy and ominous. "What is it?" I prompt, a knot of dread tightening in my stomach.

She swallows hard, her next words coming out in a rush, "Mr. Dreschel died in a car accident last night. We're all in shock."

The words hit me like a physical blow, leaving me momentarily breathless. Frank Dreschel—the man who was supposed to help me navigate through the murky waters of my family's legacy—gone just like that in a freak car accident? It doesn't seem possible.

I stand there, stunned, trying to process the news. Questions swirl through my mind, each one more urgent than the last. Who else knows about the will? Was it really an accident, or is there more to the story, especially given the danger that has been surrounding me lately? And, most importantly, what do I do now?

Trying to keep my voice as steady as possible, I lean in slightly, doing my best to come off as non-threatening. "Do you know if Mr. Dreschel... did he find out anything about my father's will?"

The receptionist bites her lip, clearly torn. After a moment, she nods, reluctantly admitting, "Yes, he did. He was here late last night, working on it. Something about the will caught his interest, and whatever it was, he seemed to think it was important." Her voice trails off, and she looks away, adding, "He was on his way home from here when the accident happened."

She shakes her head in disbelief. "His car was brand-new," she says. "And yet the police say the brakes failed. It's all so strange. Everything about it is just... off."

Part of me wants to leave, so I don't risk upsetting the receptionist more than she already is. But the greater part of me understands this is an opportunity I can't waste. "Would it be possible for me to take a look at the information he found?" I ask, trying to sound hopeful rather than desperate.

The receptionist hesitates, a silent battle playing out behind her eyes. Finally, she sighs, resignation etched into her features. "I suppose. Mr. Dreschel mentioned he was planning to call you first thing this morning. As I said, he seemed to think whatever he'd found was important, something you needed to know about right away." She stands up, moving toward a file cabinet with a reluctance that tells me she's stepping out of her comfort zone.

I follow her, my heart pounding. As she hands me a file, our eyes meet—an unspoken understanding passing between us. We're both in uncharted waters here, but it's clear she's choosing to trust Mr. Dreschel's judgment, even in the aftermath of his sudden death.

The receptionist ushers me into a small, somewhat sterile conference room. "I'll be right back," she says before offering me a seat and then exiting, clicking the door shut behind her. The air feels charged like it's brimming with secrets just waiting to spill over. She returns shortly, carrying a manila folder.

"Here's everything Mr. Dreschel was reviewing. Please, try not to take too long," she says, her voice low, almost a whisper as if tremendous consequences await if I do.

As soon as the door clicks shut behind her, I dive into the folder like it's the last lifeboat off a sinking ship. The will is there, just as promised, but it's a sea of legal jargon and highlighted sections that make my head spin.

Also nestled among the documents is Mr. Dreschel's note-book, a chaotic collection of handwritten comments and observations that seem to jump off the page with urgency.

I take a deep breath and start sifting through the documents, my brain working overtime to keep up with the legal speak.

Hereunto, the party of the first part shall bequeath unto the party of the second part, I mutter under my breath, sounding like I've swallowed a law textbook.

But slowly, piece by piece, the riddles begin to make sense. And then the reality of what I'm reading hits me. According to the will, Sharon stands to inherit everything, every last dime of my father's money that's been sitting in a trust, *should anything happen to me.*

My hands shake as I flip through Mr. Dreschel's notes, his handwriting a mess of loops and scribbles that somehow make more sense than the legal documents.

Potential conflict of interest. Questionable motives. Review trust conditions and clauses regarding beneficiary designation.

Each note is a breadcrumb leading me down the path to the witch's cottage, a path I'm not sure I want to follow.

The implications are staggering. It's not just about the money—though, the stakes are high there—it's the betrayal, the undercurrents of greed and manipulation that seem to underpin this entire situation.

How could Sharon be the beneficiary? And, more importantly, why? Was this a setup from the start? Is it a game with me as the unwitting pawn?

The most likely scenario is that Sharon strong-armed Dad into it. Or had her lawyer change things around when Dad was incapacitated before his death. She'd had power of attorney, after all.

I close the folder, my mind racing with questions. I'm caught right in the middle of this mess, trying to piece together a mystery that seems to deepen with every discovery.

The receptionist's earlier words echo in my mind, urging me to hurry. I need more time and more information, but I don't have the luxury of digging deeper right now.

Letting out a heavy sigh, I feel the full weight of the situation. It's like I've been walking through a dense fog that's suddenly lifted to reveal a landscape far more treacherous than I'd ever imagined. The pieces slot together with chilling clarity—Sharon, with her almost cartoonish villainy, is not just a thorn in my side—she's a direct threat to my life.

I power up my phone, bracing myself for the avalanche of missed calls and messages. I call Elena back and she picks up before the first ring even finishes, her voice full of irritation and concern. "Maura, where the hell are you? I've been worried sick!"

I cut straight to the chase, the urgency of the situation leaving no room for small talk. "Elena, listen, I found out something huge. It's about my father's will, and it could tie into the failed assassination attempts."

Elena's initial annoyance quickly turns to worry. "Oh my God, Maura. That sounds terrifying."

"It is. It looks like my stepmother is behind the attempts on my life. And she stands to gain everything if she succeeds." Saying it out loud makes it all the more real and all the more shocking.

Elena is silent for a moment. "Maura, this is serious. You're in more danger than we thought. You need to get back to the mansion—now."

"I know; I'm calling an Uber as we speak. I'll be there as fast as I can," I assure her, my fingers already navigating through the app to summon a ride.

"No way. Send me your pin, and the bodyguards will come and get you. I'll call a car to pick me up here. Don't go anywhere else; stay right where you are, okay?" Elena's voice is dripping with urgency and concern, a stark reminder of the risks.

"I will do that. And Elena? Thanks for being there," I add, feeling a surge of gratitude for her unwavering support in this whirlwind of madness.

"Of course. You're family, remember? Stubborn, disobedient family, but family nonetheless." I can hear her smile through the phone.

In a frantic race against time, I snap photos of the will and Mr. Dreschel's notes, my phone's camera clicking quietly in the tense silence of the room. Each image captures more of the puzzle, clues to the treachery that's been woven around me. The receptionist's return snaps me back to the present, her gentle reminder that my time is up echoing ominously in the room.

"Thank you so much for letting me review this," I manage to say, handing back the folder and offering my condolences on Mr. Dreschel's untimely passing. I step into the elevator and descend back into the world with a heavy heart.

As the floors tick by, a chilling thought worms its way into my mind. What if Sharon and Rory had something to do with Mr. Dreschel's death? The idea that they could go to such lengths, eliminating anyone who gets too close to the truth, sends a shiver down my spine.

My heart races, not just with fear, but with the desperate need to be back at the mansion, safe in Luk's arms, to share with him the news of our baby.

The lobby passes in a blur as I make my way outside, my eyes scanning for the bodyguards and our car. The sight of a familiar, black car with dark-tinted windows parked curbside sends a wave of relief through me, and I hurriedly open the back door and slip inside, not giving the driver a chance to open it for me. My relief is short-lived as I slide into the backseat and come face to face with my nightmare—Sharon—smirking like the cat that ate the canary, with Rory in the driver's seat ominously silent.

Sharon's voice is silk over steel. "Maura, darling, so very pleased you could join us."

Panic grips me as I reach for the door, only to find it locked. Rory doesn't say a word; he simply pulls away from the curb, sealing my fate. Before we get too far, he reaches back with surprising speed and plucks my phone out of my hand, tossing it out the window with a quick snap of his wrist.

I'm trapped, my heart pounding in my chest as the car speeds away. Every instinct screams at me to fight, to find a way out, knowing that with every turn, I'm getting farther from safety, farther from Luk.

Sharon watches me, her gaze wicked and calculating. "You've been a busy bee, Maura. Digging into things that you shouldn't be. We can't have that, now, can we?"

Her words are cold, a clear reminder of the danger I've stumbled into. It's not just about the inheritance anymore; it's about survival. The cruelty Sharon showed me throughout most of my life has followed me into adulthood, into marriage, and into the life I swore to keep her out of.

I weigh my options, desperate for any leverage, any angle to use against them. But Sharon's smug grin and Rory's silent compliance tell me I'm at a disadvantage.

I realize that this is it—the confrontation I've been dreading. But I'm not the same frightened woman I was when I married Luk two months ago. And I have more to fight for now than ever before.

CHAPTER 23

LUK

Tonight, the mansion feels more like a fortress, each tick of the clock amplifying the silence. I'm pacing the expansive living room when Elena bursts through the door.

Without missing a beat, I launch into her. "Where the hell have you been? And where's Maura? I asked you to keep an eye on her, Elena."

Elena, completely unfazed by my towering frustration, raises an eyebrow and places her purse on the console with exaggerated care. "First of all, Luk, you need to calm down. And second, Maura's not a child that needs constant supervision. She went to try and solve this enigma, to figure out who is behind the attempts on her life. She's taking matters into her own hands."

The defiance in her tone and the challenge in her eyes only serve to stoke the fire already burning in my belly. They also force me to confront a fact I've been avoiding. Maura's spirit, her dogged pursuit of the truth, is part of what draws me to her. It's a trait I admire, even when it scares the hell out of me.

"She's definitely headstrong," I concede, my voice gruff with pride and concern. "But this isn't some game. The stakes are life and death. She shouldn't be facing this alone. And I don't, in the slightest, appreciate her evading you and the guards to run off on her own—yet again."

Elena crosses her arms, standing her ground as if she's the older sibling schooling me. "Maura doesn't back down, not from you, not from anyone. It's one of her strengths."

I want to argue that there's a difference between self-assurance and recklessness, but Elena's jawline tells me she's not done.

"And you love her for it," she continues, softer now but with no less intensity. "She's out there because she can't stand the thought of anyone else getting hurt. Not you, not me, not anyone. Maura's fighting for us as much as for herself."

I feel the heat of my anger cooling in the face of Elena's unwavering logic. She's right, damn her.

"But her phone's off. What if something's happened to her?" The worry that's been gnawing at me breaks free, coloring my voice with fear.

Elena's expression softens, her earlier fire replaced by genuine concern. "Hmm, that's odd. But she's smart. Maura knows what she's doing, and she's on her way home now. The guards picked her up a little bit ago."

Her words, meant to be reassuring, only serve to underscore the urgency of the situation. Maura is out there yet I'm in here. My place is by her side, protecting her, fighting alongside her.

"Maura's competency isn't the issue. The fact of the matter is that there are people out there who want to kill her. I need to find her."

As I turn to leave, Elena's voice stops me cold. "What's your plan? Are you going to tear down the whole of Chicago to track her down? I already told you. She's on her way here; the guards have her."

I pause, realizing that in my rush of fear and anger, I hadn't thought things through. "I can't just sit here, wait, and do nothing," I admit, the words tasting like defeat.

Elena nods, a knowing look in her eyes as if she'd been expecting such a moment. "Come with me to my computer room."

I follow her through the mansion to a room that starkly contrasts with the rest of the opulent decor. Elena's command center is a tech enthusiast's dream—a sleek, modern setup with multiple monitors displaying various data streams, a high-end computer system that hums quietly in the background, and an array of gadgets that would be more at home in a spy movie than in a Chicago mansion.

"What is all this?" I ask.

Elena, booting up her systems, doesn't look up. "Let's just say I've got a few tricks up my sleeve. Now, let's see how close she is."

Elena's fingers fly over the keyboard; her focus is absolute as she navigates through screens with practiced ease. I watch, feeling oddly out of my element in this digital realm she commands so effortlessly.

"Maura was digging into her father's will. She shared with me that she discovered something troubling. It seems Sharon stands to inherit everything if Maura is out of the picture," Elena says, her voice steady despite the gravity of her words.

A cold fury settles in my chest, a confirmation of my darkest suspicions. "Sharon's been suspect number one all along in my book. But I needed hard proof," I tell her.

Elena pauses her work, turning to face me with a serious look. "It sounds like Maura might've found exactly that, which means Sharon just became even more dangerous."

The mere thought of Sharon acting on her vile intentions, of Maura being in danger because she came too close to the truth, ignites a boiling rage within me. My fists clench at my sides with the need for action and retribution.

"She should have been home by now. I don't have a good feeling about this, Elena," I growl, the words barely containing my anger.

Elena nods, her expression grim but determined. "I'm on it. I have a few ways to track phones, even if they're turned off."

As Elena gets back to work, studying her screen full of codes and maps, I'm forced to stand back, my self-control slipping through my fingers like sand. I'm not the leader of a vast empire at the moment, not the alpha who commands respect and fear. I'm a man terrified for the woman he loves, rendered nearly powerless by the plotting of a greedy, vindictive adversary.

"What exactly are you doing?" I ask, my impatience getting the better of me as I watch Elena's concentrated effort on the screen.

"I'm tracking the last known location of Maura's phone," she responds, not looking away from her task. "I've installed heavy-duty encryption on all of our phones for protection. Even though I designed it, breaking through is going to take a minute."

I'm torn between admiring her foresight and frustrated at the delay. My gaze is glued to the screen, and my body is taut with anticipation.

After what feels like an eternity, the screen shifts, displaying a detailed map of Chicago with a small, blinking dot in the center. "There she is," Elena announces with a hint of relief in her voice. "Or was."

She zooms in, the dot unmoving on a street near a towering skyscraper downtown. "What does this mean?" I demand, my heart rate spiking.

"It means her phone was turned off here—or it was left behind," Elena explains, her tone somber.

My gut clenches with a familiar dread. This isn't a good sign, not by any stretch. The location, the sudden silence from Maura's phone—it all paints a grim picture.

Just then, the two bodyguards assigned to escort her and keep her safe burst into the room. "Mr. Ivanov, sir, we have a situation."

"We need to move—now!" I say without giving them time to explain. "Gather a team. We're going there."

"Hold on," Elena says, her fingers poised above the keyboard.

"What is it?" I ask through gritted teeth, barely managing to keep the fury out of my voice.

"I'm going to hack into the traffic cameras around that location. Maybe we can spot something useful," she explains.

I nod, giving my silent assent. "Do it."

Elena's expertise comes to the forefront as she navigates through layers of security with calm efficiency. Within minutes, she's in, and the live feeds from several traffic cameras fill the screen. I can't help but express my admiration. "I'm impressed," I admit, watching her work.

She shoots me a quick wink, not slowing down for a second. "You haven't seen anything yet."

We watch the screens intently, Elena rewinding the footage to the moments after Maura's last call. My heart races as Maura's figure emerges from the building. She moves quickly—her urgency is evident even in the grainy footage—and heads straight for a black car that pulls up to the curb, one that looks very similar to our security sedans.

"There!" I point at the screen. "Zoom in on that car."

Elena obliges, enhancing the image until the details become clearer. The man behind the wheel comes into focus, and a cold rage settles over me as I recognize Rory.

"Sharon has her," I hiss, the realization hitting me like a physical blow.

Elena looks at me, her expression bleak. "What's our next move, Luk?"

I take a second, my mind racing. "We're going after them. We're going to get my wife back, no matter what it takes."

I grab my phone, dial my men, and give a command that brooks no argument. "Prepare for an assault. No holds barred; no quarter given. We're bringing her back by any means necessary." My tone is pure steel, leaving no room for questions or hesitation.

I walk past the two guards as I leave Elena's tech room. Looking each straight in the eye, I tell them, "We will discuss what happened today at a later time. Right now, I need you to gear up and help me get her back."

I head straight to the war room, rightfully named for what is kept within its walls. I strap on my vest and choose my weapons carefully, loading each one and cocking them, ensuring the safety is on once I do so. As I pack extra ammunition into my cargo pants, a torrent of emotions crashes over me. It's in this moment of clarity, amid the storm of preparation, that I truly understand the depth of my love for Maura. The thought that I hadn't fully acknowledged these feelings before, that I could lose her without ever having fully embraced that truth, gnaws at me with a ferocity that's almost too much to bear.

Fully equipped, I step out of the war room, only to find Elena waiting for me, her expression taut.

"What is it?" I ask, sensing the urgency of whatever she's holding back. "Tell me."

Elena exhales heavily. "There's something you need to know. Something I swore to keep secret, to let her tell you herself, but it's too important to keep from you."

Impatience and worry twist inside me, a volatile mix that threatens to explode. "Out with it."

She meets my gaze, her resolve crumbling under the weight of her next words. "Maura's pregnant, Luk."

The world seems to stop for a moment; the news takes my breath away. *Pregnant*? Maura is carrying our child, and she's out there, in danger, because of Sharon.

The stakes, already sky-high, catapult into the stratosphere. This isn't just about saving the woman I love anymore; it's about protecting our future, our family.

I steel myself, the newfound knowledge fueling a fierce determination within me. "Do or die," I whisper, more to myself than to Elena, vowing to bring Maura home, no matter the cost.

Elena nods, her eyes reflecting the gravity of the situation. "We're with you. The family's with you."

I head down the hall, every step purposeful. The mission is clear, and the objective is singular. Rescue Maura and ensure the safety of our unborn child.

There is no other option.

CHAPTER 24

MAURA

Fear and anger churn within me as I sit trapped in the back of the car. The cold, metallic glint of Sharon's gun is a constant reminder of the direness of my situation. Rory's eyes meet mine in the rearview mirror, but Sharon's smug satisfaction fuels my growing rage. The silence stretches oppressively and heavily until I can't bear it any longer.

"Why are you doing this?" I spit out, my voice laced with fear and fury. "What makes you think you have the right to tear apart my family, to take what my father rightfully left for me?"

Sharon's laughter fills the car, a sound devoid of warmth or genuine enjoyment. She turns to me, the gun still pointed in my direction, her eyes alight with a cruel glee. "Oh, Maura, do you not understand how the law works? I married your father. That means whatever he had should rightly go to me. I earned it, after all."

Her words are like a slap in the face, a twisted justification for her greed and malice. The absurdity of her claim, her belief that she's entitled to the fruits of a life and a family she had no part in building, ignites a fire within me.

"Earned it? By doing what, Sharon? By scheming and plotting? You think marriage entitles you to things that were never meant for you?" My voice rises, the anger boiling over despite the danger of provoking her further.

Sharon's smirk widens, the barrel of the gun cold against my skin. "Yes, I believe I have earned it. That's how the world works, sweetheart. Your father was a fool, blinded by sentiment. I simply recognized that and swooped in, taking advantage of the situation. But a fool, I'm not. I see things clearly. I take what I want, and what I want is everything he left behind. *Everything.*"

Her words send a chill down my spine, and I'm reminded of the ruthless world I'm entangled in. But even in the face of her wickedness, I feel a resolve forming within, a strength I didn't know I had. I may be at her mercy right now, but I'm not defeated. Not yet.

"You won't get away with this," I tell her, meeting her gaze with defiance. "There are people who will come for me, who will stop at nothing to see you pay for what you've done."

Sharon's response is an evil and dismissive laugh. "Let them try. I've always been one step ahead. And soon, everything will be mine."

The car speeds on, the city a colorful blur beyond the windows. But inside the moving prison, I'm trapped in a battle of wills rages. Sharon may think she has the upper hand, but I'm not alone in this fight. I've no doubt Luk is moving heaven and earth to find me.

The tension in the back of the car is so thick you could cut it with a knife. Rory continues to drive in silence, his focus is unwavering, while Sharon keeps her gun trained on me, a twisted smile playing on her lips. Fear claws at my insides, but it's the fury, the burning sense of injustice, that propels me forward.

I'm shocked when Rory suddenly speaks. He's always been the silent type, the muscle behind Sharon's schemes. Now, he speaks up with a passion I've never seen him display. "We've waited decades for this," he says, sounding almost giddy. "We finally have the means to be together openly. With Mick's money, it will no longer be a dream; it will be our reality."

Sharon's expression softens at his words, and she reaches forward to gently brush his cheek with her hand, a gesture of intimacy that makes my skin crawl.

"You're both so selfish," I spit out, the disgust thick in my voice. "You're willing to destroy innocent lives for your own gains."

But my words don't reach them. They're locked in their own world, convinced of their righteousness. It's then that the horrifying realization dawns on me—not only do they intend to kill me, but they genuinely believe they'll get away with it.

Panic turns to fury, then back to panic again, a dangerous cocktail that has me searching desperately for a way out. But with Rory at the wheel and Sharon's gun never wavering, my options are limited. I have to be smart, to wait for the right moment.

An intense feeling of desperation claws at me, suffocating me. In a moment of sheer panic, grasping at straws, I take a deep breath and play my last card. "Sharon," I say, trying to control the tremble in my voice, "I'm pregnant."

I watch her closely, searching for any signs of humanity, any flicker of compassion, but what I find is anything but. Her hateful amusement only deepens, her smile stretching into a grotesque mimicry of joy. "Maura," she purrs, her voice dripping with mock sympathy, "that just makes this all the sweeter. Taking you out now means ending the Flanagan line for good and robbing Luk of not just a wife but an heir."

Her words ignite something primal within me, and I lunge at her. But Sharon is quick and strong. She dodges my clumsy attack with ease, her movements precise and quick. Before I know it, she's overpowered me, my arms secured behind my back with zip ties that bite into my skin.

Panting, my heart racing with fear and thwarted rage, I realize the gravity of my mistake. I've played my hand and lost, leaving myself even more vulnerable than before. The hope that my news might have swayed Sharon now seems foolish. She's beyond reason, beyond compassion.

As Rory drives on, oblivious or indifferent to the struggle in the back seat, I'm left to confront the grim reality of my situation. I'm at Sharon's mercy. The only thing left to do is wait and hope that Luk finds me before it's too late—for me and our unborn child.

We drive farther from the city, the landscape shifting from the familiar urban sprawl to a more desolate, industrial scene. The buildings grow sparse, replaced by factories and abandoned warehouses. Through the tinted windows, the world outside looks increasingly bleak.

I can't help but notice Rory's repeated glances in the rearview mirror. There's something in his expression that I can't quite place—worry, maybe even fear. It's odd to see any sign of doubt on the face of someone who's always seemed so unshakable in their loyalty to my evil stepmother.

Eventually, we pull up to a rundown warehouse, the kind of place where, just as in horror movies, nothing good ever happens. The sky has darkened, and the first drops of rain begin to patter against the car windows. Through the window, I see that Sharon's men are already at the warehouse, forming a small welcoming party of sorts. They are all heavily armed and looking a little too eager for what's to come.

Sharon steps out of the car with a look of satisfaction on her face, as if everything is going exactly according to her plan. I'm pulled roughly from the car, my heart pounding in my chest, not just for myself but for the baby. The idea of Luk bursting through the doors, guns blazing, is the only thought keeping me from total despair.

Yet, as the minutes tick by, the reality of my situation sinks in. I'm at the mercy of a woman who sees my death as the key to her happiness and surrounded by men who won't hesitate to carry out her orders. These men believe the bullshit promises she's no doubt given them.

The hope that Luk will find me, that he'll come to my rescue, feels more and more like a distant dream.

But it's that sliver of hope, thin as it may be, that I cling to. For my sake and the baby's, I have to believe that Luk is out there searching for me, that he'll find me before it's too late. The thought of not seeing him again, of our child growing up without a mother—or worse, not growing up at all—is too much to bear.

So I pray that Luk's love for me is strong enough to lead him here, to this godforsaken place, in time.

Rory hauls me into the empty warehouse. It's dark and eerie and smells like death. However, I'm not about to go down without a fight, so the second we're inside, I run. But Sharon's hired muscle is on me before I get far.

They tie me to a chair, and it becomes crystal clear that unless Luk turns up—and fast—this could be it for me. That thought alone is enough to kick my survival instincts into overdrive. I need to stall, to buy some time, any way I can.

And then it hits me. Sharon loves nothing more than the sound of her own voice, especially when she's rambling on about her grand plans and twisted justifications. As she starts her usual spiel, taunting me with that smug look in her eyes, a lightbulb goes off in my head.

"Sharon," I start, my voice neutral despite the turmoil raging inside me. "You've always got so much to say about your plans, your reasons. How about you enlighten me? After all, it's not like I'm going anywhere."

It's a Hail Mary, but if I can keep her talking, keep her distracted, maybe I can buy Luk the time he needs to find me. So I brace myself, ready to dive into the depths of Sharon's ego if it means a shot at getting out alive.

Sharon chuckles like she's genuinely amused. "Desperate to cling on to your last moments, huh?" she muses, like she's enjoying this twisted scenario. Deciding to indulge her own ego, she launches into her spiel. "You see, Maura, a little brat like you never deserved what your father built. Only someone like me, someone with real ambition, can turn what he started into a proper empire."

I can't help myself. Maybe it's the fear, the disgust toward her, or just my natural instinct to fight back with whatever I've got left, but I shoot back, "Yes, I'm not sure how blowing his cash on your wardrobe fits into empire-building, but whatever."

That clearly hits a nerve. Her eyes narrow into angry slits, and without warning, she smacks me across the face. The shock of it stings, but it's the realization that she's genuinely unhinged that turns my blood to ice.

Then she composes herself, smoothing her skirt, a prim expression taking hold. I can sense that she wasn't happy with letting me get to her like that.

Her voice takes on a chillingly calm tone as she elaborates on her grand plan, each word slicing through the stale air. "Your father's legacy was wasted on him, and it would have been wasted on you, too. But under my control, we're going to expand. The Flanagan name will be synonymous with power in Chicago. And Luk's little Bratva?" a wicked chuckle escapes her. "They'll be crushed like bugs under my heel."

I can't help but scoff at her delusions of grandeur, the absurdity of her ambition momentarily overshadowing the fear. "Really, Sharon? Do you think you can run Chicago? You can't even keep your own people in line without resorting to threats. How are you going to manage an entire city?"

My words seem to bounce off her, her focus unshaken as she revels in her own narrative. She's so caught up in her victory lap that my skepticism doesn't even register as a blip on her radar. Instead, she moves closer, her expression shifting to one of smug satisfaction as she prepares to drop what she clearly believes is her ace in the hole.

"Oh dear, naïve Maura," she says, her voice dropping to a whisper that's somehow more menacing than her earlier bravado, "there's something else you should know. Your father's untimely demise?" Her eyes lock onto mine, holding me captive to her next words. "That was my doing."

The world seems to freeze around us, the sound of rain against the metal roof fading into nothingness. Sharon's admission sends a shockwave through me, a mix of horror, disbelief, and a wave of deep, seething anger. My father's death, a wound that's never fully healed, has been reopened with a new, dark truth.

CHAPTER 25

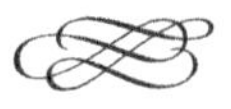

MAURA

The revelation hits me like a tidal wave, emotions crashing over me with an intensity I can't control. Tears of disbelief blur my vision. Rory watches the scene unfold with what seems like detached interest.

But for a fleeting moment, I catch something in his gaze—a flicker of sorrow, perhaps, or maybe a hint of regret. It's gone as quickly as it appeared, leaving me to wonder if I imagined it.

I struggle against the zip ties binding my wrists together, the need for answers, for understanding, pushing me beyond the physical pain and emotional turmoil. "How?" I demand. "How did you do it?"

Sharon looks almost disinterested as she basks in the glow of her own perceived cleverness. "Your father," she begins, her tone dripping with disdain, "was always too small-minded. He cared for nothing beyond his precious little territory, his neighborhood. He lacked vision and ambition. Taking him out of the equation was simple."

She pauses, a cruel smile curling her lips as she savors the moment. "All it took was ensuring his heart medication was just out of reach during one of his episodes. To everyone else, it appeared as nothing more than a tragic occurrence."

The words are a gut punch. My father—whose only crime was his dedication to his community and his family—was reduced to nothing more than an obstacle in Sharon's path.

The realization that his death—which shattered my world—was orchestrated so coldly, so calculatedly leaves me spinning.

I wish Sharon had never come into our lives.

Rage simmers beneath the surface, a burning desire to make Sharon pay for her crimes. But with my options limited, my body restrained, all I can do is listen, absorbing the weight of her confession.

"Once I'm done, the Flanagan legacy will be nothing more than a footnote in my empire. Your father was just the beginning, Maura. He was too shortsighted and too obsessed with his community to see its true potential."

"You think you can just erase us? Erase my father's life's work with a wave of your hand?"

She laughs, a sound that's both chilling and infuriating. "Of course, my dear. It's already happening. And you? You're just another loose end to tie up."

Despair threatens to consume me, but a stubborn spark of defiance ignites within. Sharon may believe she's won, that she's stripped me of everything, but she's underestimated my strength. My father's memory, the love I have for Luk, and the future of our child—will not be extinguished.

Out of the corner of my eye, I catch Rory shifting uncomfortably. I seize on it, desperate for any crack in their united front. "Even Rory doesn't seem too sure about your plan, Sharon. Or are you too blinded by your wicked ambition to notice?"

Rory remains silent, his expression unreadable, but the momentary lapse doesn't go unnoticed. Sharon seems oblivious to his hesitation; however, she is far too caught up in herself. "I know where Rory's loyalty lies. As for you, dear, your time is running out."

Sharon's face hardens, a mask of annoyance settling over her features. "Enough of this," she declares, her voice cold and commanding. "Rory, finish her, once and for all."

Rory, who's always followed Sharon's orders without question, pauses—a hesitation so slight, yet so profound. It's the first crack in his unwavering loyalty. A small smile forms on my lips at the sight.

Sharon's patience snaps like a twig. "Now, Rory. We finish this tonight," she orders, her voice laced with a heartless finality.

He shifts uncomfortably, avoiding Sharon's gaze. "She's pregnant, Sharon. It doesn't sit right with me," he admits, his voice barely above a whisper.

I seize the moment despite the fear gripping me. "Rory, you don't have to do this. There's still a chance to make this right," I urge him, attempting to take advantage of the shred of morality he's showing.

Sharon's fury boils over. "This isn't up for debate! We can't let her go. Luk will tear the city apart to find her. She's a loose end that needs to be tied up—permanently," Sharon barks, her eyes blazing with a manic intensity.

Rory looks torn. His loyalty to Sharon is at war with his moral compass. "Can't we just send her away to another country? Something similar to a witness protection program, although she'll be guarded, heavily watched," he suggests in a desperate attempt to find a middle ground.

Sharon stares at Rory for a full minute, a look of disbelief on her face. "No!" she finally shouts, her voice slicing through the silent tension. "Luk will never stop looking for her. He has... ways of getting people to talk. He'll stop at nothing to find her. And when he does, there's no telling what he'll do to us. She cannot leave here alive."

Sharon and Rory stare at one another, each one unwavering. I sit in awe at what I'm witnessing. Never before has Rory defied her, and I can see the decision weighing heavily on him, the moment stretching out like a tightrope.

Suddenly, the standoff is shattered by the sound of gunfire. The noise is deafening in the quiet of the warehouse. Sharon whirls around, startled, her momentary distraction offering a glimpse of vulnerability.

Rory's attention zeroes in on the source of the disturbance, his hand instinctively moving to his weapon. The dynamic shifts in an instant and the imminent threat from outside temporarily unites them in confusion and fear.

For a brief moment, I am forgotten, supplanted by the immediate need to respond to the unknown danger. My heart races, not knowing what this development means for me. Is it a rescue or a new threat?

One of the guards, holding a mean-looking assault rifle in his hands, rushes into the warehouse.

"It's Ivanov," he says. "He's found us."

It's all I can do to keep from shouting with joy. "How?" The word explodes from Sharon's mouth. "How the hell did he find us?"

The guard shrugs in response.

Sharon screams in frustration. "Rory, the two of you go up to the second floor and take out as many as you can."

Rory and the guard obey, and the crackle of gunfire grows louder and closer. Sharon rushes toward one of the windows, her small pistol in hand, as she assesses the situation.

Unbeknownst to Sharon, while she and Rory have their lovers' quarrel, I manage to wriggle my hands free from the ties. Touching my belly, I remind myself it's not just about me anymore. I've got a tiny, second heartbeat to think about now, and I have to get to safety.

I place my hands back behind the chair so as not to tip Sharon off that I've freed myself. As I glance around the space, I spot a large, damaged vent on a far wall. It's a long shot, but it might just be my ticket to dodging bullets and protecting myself and my unborn child. If I can get over there and shimmy the vent cover free, I might be able to hoist myself up and out.

With Sharon preoccupied at the window, I slowly sneak toward the vent, hoping that the noise from the gunfire covers up any sounds getting the vent off the wall might make. Luck is on my side, as I'm able to pry the cover off in a matter of seconds. Just as I'm about to make my move and heave myself up into it, Sharon snaps her gaze away from the window and catches me in the act. "Really, Maura?" she says with annoyance, catching my eye. "You think you can get away that easily?"

It has now become a standoff between me and my evil stepmother. My heart's racing, knowing I've got to make a move immediately. "Watch me," I tell her, trying to sound braver than I feel.

It's do or die.

I lunge for the vent, the idea of defeating her giving me a burst of energy. Sharon's hot on my heels as I squeeze myself through the opening. I desperately pull myself forward in an army crawl, trying to get my feet to safety before she can pull me back out by them.

The sounds of the fight outside are a stark reminder of what Luk's risking to save me. I can't let that be for nothing.

Freedom is just one more elbow in front of the other when I feel it—the cold grip of Sharon's hand on my foot. Panic and survival immediately take hold. "Let go!" I yell, thrashing and kicking to free myself from her hold.

Sharon's not giving up, though, and for a second, it feels like I'm done. But then adrenaline kicks in, and I lash out once again, harder this time, my foot connecting with her face. She stumbles back, giving me exactly the time I need to get into a safe space in the vent.

As I continue to crawl through the tight space, every move is fueled by sheer willpower. I emerge on the second floor, gasping for breath, only to find myself facing a new nightmare. Sharon's goons are everywhere, their guns trained on the windows, ready for Luk and his crew. My heart sinks. So much for my grand escape.

As much as I hate to admit it, I'm cornered, and I can't take on Sharon and her army of thugs alone.

I hunker down, trying to stay out of sight. I can't help but feel like some cliché damsel in distress waiting for her hero to burst through the door. And as much as that grates on me, that's kind of what I am, but thank God Luk's coming.

"Come on, Luk," I whisper under my breath, more a prayer than anything else. "It's all on you now."

The sound of gunfire and the chaos below only heighten my anxiety. I'm trapped, but I'm not out of the fight—not yet. If Luk has taught me anything, it's that there's always a way out, always another move to make. So, I will wait, ready to do whatever I can to help, to make sure that when he does burst through those doors, we're ready to take Sharon down together.

I don't have to wait long, though; unfortunately, it isn't Luk who finds me.

CHAPTER 26

LUK

The scent of gunpowder fills the air as we approach the perimeter of the warehouse. My crew—Lev, Grigori, Elena, Yuri, and a squad of our best and most trusted men—moves like a well-oiled machine, our steps synchronized as we move in. Gunfire continues to erupt around us in a malicious symphony as we dive headlong into the fray.

"Lev left flank! Grigori, you're with me. Yuri, cover our six!" I shout, my voice cutting through the noise as we advance, bullets whizzing past us. Sharon's goons are putting up a fight, but they're scattered, their fire erratic. It's clear they weren't prepared for a full-on Bratva assault.

Elena, ever the sharpshooter, takes out a shooter on the roof, her precision unmatched. "Got him," she calls out, a hint of satisfaction in her tone.

"Keep the pressure on! They're breaking!" I yell, rallying my family and our heavies. We're a storm—relentless and unforgiving—closing in on Sharon's last line of defense.

But just as we're tightening the noose, Elena's urgent and grave voice cuts through the commotion. "Luk, we've got trouble!" she shouts, ducking for cover as she waves her phone at me.

I make my way over to her, bullets zinging past. "What's going on?" I demand, the rhythm of my heart syncing with the rapid fire around us.

Elena's expression is dismal, her eyes locked on mine. "It's Sharon—I'm listening in on her line. She's called in reinforcements, a lot of them. They're on their way."

The news hits like a ton of bricks, and the brief taste of victory I was tasting turns sour. We're outnumbered but not outmatched—not yet. My mind races, strategizing, calculating our next move in milliseconds. "All right, listen up!" I bark to my crew, my voice calm but filled with deadly intent. "They're coming for a fight," I call out, reloading my weapon. "Let's give them one they won't forget."

The anticipation of the approaching enemy tightens the air, the warehouse a battlefield set for a clash where both sides will fight to the death. We're ready, each of us prepared to lay it all on the line—for family, for honor, and love.

Grigori and I move with purpose, our steps calculated and swift, as we circle around to the side of the building. The air is electric, charged with the imminent threat of conflict. Just as we round the corner, one of Sharon's men, thinking he's got the drop on us, steps out, gun raised.

He doesn't stand a chance.

Grigori's on him in a heartbeat, a silent shadow closing the gap. The guy barely has time to register his surprise before

Grigori's hands are on him. A swift, precise strike to the throat stifles any cry for help; a follow-up knee to the gut has him doubled over. Grigori finishes with a sharp twist, an arm lock that causes the man to hit the ground hard. He's disarmed and neutralized in seconds. The first of Sharon's reinforcements make their appearance from the back, a ragtag crew thinking they're about to turn the tide. They're met with Grigori's unyielding defense, his gunfire a relentless barrage that pins them down. "Keep them busy!" I call out, leaving him to hold the line.

I slip into the warehouse, the sounds of the battle outside fading as I step into the lion's den. It's eerily quiet inside—too quiet. I walk forward, every sense heightened, ready for whatever comes next.

The interior of the warehouse is a maze of crates and shadows, a perfect spot to stage an ambush. I move carefully, my gun at the ready, scanning for any sign of Sharon or her thugs. My heart pounds not just from the adrenaline of the fight but also from the knowledge that Maura's somewhere in this place, depending on me to get her out.

I can almost feel Sharon's malignant presence. She's close—I can sense it. She's taken something irreplaceable from me, and I'm here to take it back.

I walk farther into the warehouse, the silence shattered by the occasional crack of gunfire from Grigori. He's breached the concrete jungle. Briefly, I take comfort in knowing he's inside. Each shot is a reminder that we're running out of time; however, the enemy is at our doorstep. I push forward, driven by the need to end this, to rescue Maura and get my crew out safely, and to make sure Sharon pays for every transgression.

Grigori approaches silently and flanks me with a silent nod. We press on, methodically clearing section after section of the warehouse. Every corner we turn, every shadow we check, could be hiding death, but we move forward, undeterred. The goons are tough, but they're no match for the Bratva's might. I can feel the tide turning in our favor, the confidence in our victory mounting with each man we take down.

And then, as if summoned by my resolve, they appear—more of Sharon's thugs, lurking in the dim light of the second floor, guns drawn, ready to defend their fallen empire to the last.

But they're not ready for what I'm about to bring.

The first man doesn't even see me coming as I approach swiftly and silently from behind. One precise strike to the back of the head, and he's down, unconscious, before he hits the ground. I move again before his comrades can react, sliding between shadows like a phantom.

Another man rounds a corner, gun raised, but he's too slow. With two steps, I'm on him, disarming him with a practiced twist of his arm that leaves him yelping in pain. I give one quick jab to the temple, and he joins his buddy on the floor, out cold.

The way I move through them is methodical, almost mechanical. Each takedown is a message carved in silence and shadow. I'm the predator, the reaper in the dark. Each fallen man is a testament to my promise, my resolve to protect what's mine.

The warehouse may be their territory, but I've turned it into my hunting ground. With every man who drops, I'm one step closer to Maura, one step closer to ending this nightmare. Sharon's minions may have thought they were the hunters, but they've quickly learned that they're the prey.

I make my way onto the roof with Grigori close behind me, backing me up. Sharon, venomous as ever, stands there next to Maura, who's a picture of defiance despite her perilous situation. Rory is also there. He's a mountain of a man who is barely containing the rage that brews within him. He turns his fury toward me.

Without a word, he charges, a human juggernaut fueled by loyalty or madness or perhaps both—I can't tell which. The fight is on, a clash of raw power against trained precision. Rory's size makes him formidable, but in the tight space of the rooftop, it also makes him predictable.

He swings, a move that would incapacitate any normal man, but I'm already a step ahead, ducking under his arm, using his momentum against him. The dance of combat is brutal—Rory's strength versus my agility—a test of endurance I cannot afford to lose.

With a feint and pivot, I exploit an opening, landing a series of strikes designed to disorient. Rory staggers, his resilience waning, but he's relentless, coming back at me with an almost admirable ferocity.

The decisive moment comes unexpectedly—a misstep from Rory, perhaps born of his blinding rage or sheer exhaustion. Seizing the chance, I maneuver him toward the edge; his own momentum carries him forward. With a final push, Rory's hulking frame tumbles over the edge and to the ground.

Sharon is clearly shocked by her lover's defeat. But I'm ready to finish the fight. I remove my weapon from its holster and train it directly on Sharon's forehead.

"You're too late, Luk!" Sharon sneers, her voice a twisted melody of assumed triumph and threat. "Drop your weapon, or I'll kill her." She presses the barrel of her gun to Maura's temple; I want to take her apart limb from limb.

Maura, always defiant and strong, meets my gaze with fierce determination. "Don't listen to her, Luk," she says, her voice steady but betraying none of the fear she must be feeling.

I keep my gun trained on Sharon, weighing my options in a fraction of a second. "Let her go, Sharon. This ends now," I demand, my voice a low growl.

Sharon's laugh is hollow and devoid of humanity. "You think you've won, Luk? I still hold the cards here. Make one move, and she's dead."

But Maura's not one to be underestimated. In a swift motion, she elbows Sharon in the ribs, creating just enough space between them. "Luk, now!" she shouts, seizing the moment that Sharon's distracted.

It's all the opening I need. I fire my weapon, the shot echoing across the rooftop. The bullet finds its mark, blasting the gun from Sharon's hand and sending it skittering across the concrete.

Maura doesn't hesitate. She runs straight to me, her relief visible even in the midst of the madness. I wrap an arm around her, pulling her in close, my gun still trained on Sharon.

"It's over," I say, my voice devoid of any emotion, my tone as hard as steel. The gun remains steady in my hand, continuing to relay a clear message. "You don't hold the cards, Sharon. You've lost."

CHAPTER 27

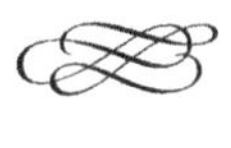

LUK

Sharon continues to stare at me with an evil glare. "Give it up. There's nowhere to go," I state as I lock eyes with her. I can tell the fight's gone out of her, leaving a desperate, cornered animal in its wake.

Sharon, even in defeat, continues to spit venom. "You think this is over?" she asks, her voice laced with arrogance. "I'll always be just around the corner, in the shadows. You and your precious family will never be safe."

I'm seething, every muscle tensed, ready to end this threat permanently. "I should just finish you now," I growl, overwhelmed by the urge to protect my family from any future harm.

Maura, sensing my intent, gently touches my arm. "No, Luk. No more violence," she pleads, her voice a beacon of reason breaking through the storm raging within me. "No more bloodshed today. Please."

Her voice and presence pull me back to sanity, quelling the tempest inside just enough. "She tried to take everything from us and nearly did. She threatened our future," I say, struggling with the weight of my emotions and the compelling urge to put a bullet through Sharon's head.

"I know, but this isn't the way. We have to be bigger than her and make better choices," Maura insists, her eyes meeting mine, a world of wisdom and compassion in her gaze.

Taking a deep breath, I make my decision, my gaze locked on Sharon. "Tell your men to stand down, drop their weapons, and leave. Do that, and I'll let you live."

Sharon appears stunned at first. Her eyes are filled with a calculating hesitation as she weighs her options.

Finally, she nods, a begrudging acknowledgment of her defeat. "Fine," she spits out, appearing disinterested in the matter as she smooths her blouse. "I'll call them off."

I keep my gun trained on her as she makes the call, her voice a reluctant murmur into her phone, instructing her remaining men to stand down and scatter. The orders are met with confusion judging by the sounds of chaos below, but bit by bit, the commotion begins to fade.

Maura squeezes my hand, silently thanking me for choosing mercy over vengeance. It wasn't easy, but her influence and her hope for a brighter path guided me to make the right choice.

"You're going to pay for this, Sharon, not with your life, but with your freedom. You're going to jail for a very, very long time," I tell her, my voice firm and confident, leaving no room for negotiation.

Sharon laughs, a brittle yet defiant sound. "You think the cops will listen to you? You're nothing but underground vermin in their eyes."

I can't help but chuckle at her naivety. "Oh, Sharon, how wrong you are. They're going to do to you exactly what I ask them to do, especially seeing as they're on my payroll." The confident arrogance drains from her face as the reality of her situation sinks in.

I pull out my phone and quickly type a message to my contact within the Chicago PD.

Got a hell of a catch for you. I hit send, the text sealing Sharon's fate.

As I secure her to a pipe, ensuring she's not going anywhere, Sharon's fury becomes a living thing, her insults sharp as knives. But her words are simply background noise, empty threats from a defeated enemy.

Police sirens begin to wail in the distance. Sharon's reign of terror is over.

Maura's grip on my hand is both a lifeline and a reminder of what truly matters. I lead her away; her gratitude for choosing a path of mercy over violent retribution echoes silently between us. "Thank you for sparing her," she says quietly. "I know what she's done, but all the same..."

"All that matters now is that you're safe," I reply. There's a part of me that wants to tell her I know about the baby and our future together, but it isn't the right moment.

We rejoin the others, my heart rejoicing at the sight of them alive and well. We reigned victorious and defeated Sharon's army of evil. An immeasurable wave of relief washes over me.

Grigori steps forward, a cocky smile on his face. "We've got a few of Sharon's crew tied up. The rest took off as soon as they saw the tide turning." His report confirms it—a total victory; Sharon's treachery is over at last.

The knowledge that we've ended the threat, that Maura and our future are safe, fills me with a sense of profound relief.

The CPD cruisers pull up, their sirens and flashing lights cutting through the silence of the aftermath. I step forward to meet them. The officers are wary once they recognize me, but they step out to greet me, nonetheless. "You'll find Sharon Flanagan tied up on the roof."

The officers exchange a look. Sharon Flanagan's name clearly rings a bell. "We'll take it from here, Mr. Ivanov. Thanks for securing the situation," one of them says, the hint of a smile playing at the edge of his lips as they head into the warehouse.

It's a comfort to have Maura at my side. Her presence is calming after the chaotic events of the night. Pulling her close, I let the barriers fall, the words spilling out with a raw honesty I've rarely allowed myself to express. "I can't believe I almost lost you tonight. I've been a damn fool. I should've told you this long before now—I love you. Every moment without you feels like an eternity."

Her eyes, bright and damp with unshed tears, meet mine. Within them, I can see everything we've been through, everything we are, and everything we will be. "I love you, too, Luk. More than you could possibly know," she whispers back, her voice steady and sure.

In the embrace that follows, there's a sense of homecoming and of the storm passing and leaving in its wake a clarity and an unbreakable bond.

"Let's go home," I say. The thought of us together in front of a roaring fire is the only thing I want.

Her warm and genuine smile lights up the dark corners of my heart. "I can't think of anything better," she replies.

Together, we watch as Sharon is loaded into the back of a squad car. The anger in her eyes is profound, a silent vow of vengeance, though it's muted, powerless behind the car's barred windows. The officer nods at me.

As we walk away, leaving the chaos and the remnants of Sharon's empire behind, I feel a weight lifting. The battle is over, but our story is just beginning.

CHAPTER 28

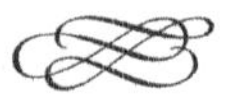

MAURA

We walk into our home just as the thunder starts rumbling. Lily practically tackles me with a hug the second we're in the door. "Oh my gosh, we were so scared!" she blurts out.

I hug her back, relishing how good it feels to be home and safe. "Thanks, Lily. It's good to be back."

"I didn't know how else to help, so I've been cooking up a storm so you would have something hot and wholesome to eat when you got back because I knew you'd be back!" With that, she runs off to the kitchen.

As we make our way through the house, Luk can't help but comment, "Seems like you're now the staff's favorite around here." He shoots me a wry smile and adds, "Guess they see in you what I do." His words warm me.

He guides me upstairs to our bedroom, where he flicks on the fireplace, instantly making the room feel cozy and warm. It's then, in the safety and sanctity of our room, with the crackling fire in the background, that the weight of the night really hits me.

I came so close to not making it home.

The realization sends a shiver through me, rattling my entire body.

Luk notices right away. In two seconds flat, he's by my side, wrapping me in his arms. It's like flipping a switch—as soon as I'm enveloped in his embrace, I feel safer, warmer, and overall better. It's his Luk magic.

"How did you even find me?" I ask, still wrapped up in his arms, the warmth from his body and the fire fighting off the last of the cold fear.

Luk chuckles, sounding a little bit proud. "Elena went full modern-day James Bond on us. Managed to hack into a GPS satellite and track the car's path. We got lucky," he admits, his eyes reflecting the flames.

Hearing that, I can't help but feel a wave of guilt crash over me. My eyes start to sting with tears—not just from relief but also from remorse. "I'm so sorry for running off like that, for being so damn reckless," I blurt out, the words come tumbling out in my haste to say them.

Luk's response is a slow nod, his eyes locking onto mine with an intensity that says he hears me; he gets it. But then he shakes his head slightly as if brushing aside my apology. "None of that matters now," he says, his voice soft but firm. "You're here, safe, in my arms. That's all I care about."

Suddenly, he's wiping away my tears, his touch gentle against my skin. He pulls me closer, and I allow myself to be held, to let his presence soothe away the last of my fears and regrets.

As we sit there, holding each other, the storm outside doesn't seem so fierce anymore. It's just the two of us in our own little sanctuary, safe from the rest of the world.

There's a deep and serious look in Luk's eyes, and it makes my heart leap. "There's something Elena told me before we got to the warehouse. She felt I needed to know before we went into battle," he says, and I know what's coming next. My stomach ties itself into knots, not from fear but from the anticipation of finally telling him about the baby.

He pauses a moment before saying, "I want to hear it from you," he says, his voice encouraging.

I take a deep breath, and feeling like I'm about to jump off a cliff, I finally spill the beans.

"I'm pregnant," I say, the words rushing out in a flood of relief and nervousness. "I wanted to tell you, I really did, but the timing never seemed right with everything that was happening. And then, when Sharon kidnapped me..."

My words trail off, hanging there between us like a delicate thread. For a second, I'm terrified he might be upset and lecture me for not telling him sooner. "Are you angry with me?" I ask, barely a whisper, bracing myself for his reaction.

Luk shakes his head, a softness in his eyes that I've only seen a few times. "Angry? Darling, I've never been happier in my life," he says, the sincerity in his voice and the tenderness in his eyes wrapping around me like a warm blanket.

All the worry and uncertainty just evaporate, leaving behind an incredible lightness. We're going to be parents, and suddenly, despite the recent chaotic events, everything feels like it's falling into place.

Luk pulls me closer, and I rest my head against his chest, listening to the steady beat of his heart.

His voice drops, embarrassment coloring his tone. "I feel like a damn fool for not telling you sooner that I loved you. So, I suppose this makes us even."

I can't help but laugh, the joyful sound bubbling up from deep within me. It's such a Luk thing to say, trying to balance the scales even in moments like this. We hold each other, wrapped up in warmth and love, as the world outside fades away.

Our eyes lock, and we share an unspoken conversation—a silent understanding that we're on the brink of something new, something amazing. Luk kisses me softly, tenderly at first, but then we're kissing deeply and passionately, trying to communicate all the love, fear, and relief of the past few hours in one moment.

I never want it to end.

CHAPTER 29

LUK

Outside the tinted windows of the sedan, I watch the overcast sky press down on the city like a heavy blanket, but there's still a hint of spring in the air, a promise of renewal and new beginnings. I'm on my way to the jail where Sharon's being held, ready to close this chapter once and for all.

However, my thoughts keep drifting back to Maura, to our future, to the little life growing inside her. Today's a big day —it's the day we find out if we're having a son or a daughter.

My phone buzzes with a text, pulling me back from my reverie.

I'm at the hospital with Elena and Lily. And yes, our personal army is here, too. I can't wait to see you later.

I can't help but smile, imagining the scene at the hospital, our extended family there for this momentous occasion. I wanted to be there, too, but Maura insisted that I make sure Sharon was out of our lives for good, and it was important to her that I go to jail.

I wish I could be there right now. I can't wait to hear all about it. Do you have any hints for me?

Her reply comes quick, laced with her characteristic playfulness.

Nice try, Mr. I-Can-Get-Anything-I-Want. You'll have to wait until you get home. No spoilers!

You're killing me here. All right, I'll play by the rules this time. I love you.

Love you, too. Hurry back!

The exchange warms me, a stark contrast to the cold formality of the task ahead. But it also reminds me of what's waiting for me once this is over, what I'm fighting for.

The car pulls up to the jail, and I steel myself for the confrontation with Sharon. I know this meeting is necessary, a final dotting of the i's and crossing of the t's in the saga she dragged us into. Yet my mind is elsewhere, with Maura and the life we're all eagerly awaiting.

With a deep breath, I step out of the car.

Striding toward the jail's entrance, my steps are measured, and my mind is a blend of anticipation and resolve. Beside me, my bodyguard keeps pace. The driver waits with the engine idling.

The jail looms before us, a stark, imposing structure of concrete and steel, the walls whispering tales of regret and retribution. The security process is thorough, the guards patting me and my bodyguard down for weapons. Metal detectors beep their cold approval as we pass, and eyes—wary and watchful—follow our every move.

Finally, we're ushered into the visiting area, a room stark in its functionality. Chairs and tables are bolted to the floor, and a glass partition is the only barrier between worlds. It's there, in a sanitized space of whispered conversations and silent prayers, that I wait for Sharon.

She arrives, a shadow of the formidable enemy we faced. Gone is the polished exterior, the confident arrogance, the carefully curated image of power and control. Instead, she's sporting the standard jail orange jumpsuit, its drabness a stark contrast to her former glory. Her face, devoid of makeup, shows the wear of sleepless nights and unyielding stress; her features are drawn, her posture slumped yet still exhibiting a small sliver of unyielding defiance.

I feel a surge of rage boil within me as she sits across from me. It's a visceral reaction, a primal response to the sight of the person who dared to threaten everything I hold dear.

"What the hell do you want?" she spits out, her voice rough, the veneer of civility long since eroded by her circumstances. Her eyes, once sharp and calculating, now burn with a combination of defiance and desperation. "You don't deserve a second of my time after what you did to me."

I can't help but offer a wry comment as Sharon settles into her seat, trying to find a comfortable position amidst the chains and handcuffs, "You're looking well," I say.

She rolls her eyes, a gesture so quintessentially Sharon, even behind the glass. "Spare me your bullshit," she retorts, her tone dripping with disdain. "Why are you here?" she presses, eager to cut through the pleasantries and get to the heart of the matter.

Leaning in, my voice is a blade of ice, "I'm here for your last words to Maura." The statement hangs between us, stark and unyielding.

Confusion flickers across her face, quickly replaced by a sneer. "Last words? Are you planning on playing executioner now, Luk?"

I shake my head slowly and deliberately. "No, Sharon. The law will handle your punishment. But you're on the hook for a laundry list of serious crimes, including murder, kidnapping, and attempted murder times two. They consider our unborn baby's life was being threatened as well when you put the gun to my wife's head. And your so-called loyal followers can't stop talking about how you murdered Maura's father. They, along with Maura, are all willing to testify that you confessed you were responsible for his death. There's a very good chance you'll be spending the rest of your life in a place much worse than this." My words are cold, a mirror reflecting the grim reality of her situation. "So, I figured I'd offer you one last chance to say something kind, show some sort of remorse for once in your life."

Her laughter is hollow, mocking. "Kind? Remorseful? You don't know me at all. I've got nothing to say to that little brat. I have no regrets about any of it."

As she scoffs at the idea, my attention is momentarily drawn to another prisoner, a thin, middle-aged woman with stringy blonde hair, making her way to the visiting booth adjacent to ours. Our eyes briefly meet, and there's a silent acknowledgment.

I quickly refocus on Sharon. "Don't get too comfortable with the idea of me rotting away in here," she taunts, leaning back comfortably as if the cold, unforgiving walls of a jail cell are not her new home. "I've got resources and plenty of money left over to pay for a top-notch legal team."

Her confidence is infuriating.

"And they're telling me there's a good chance I can cut a deal with the Feds," she continues, her smirk widening, "and that I can lessen my sentence by turning over some valuable information."

"By turning on your allies and your own son," I counter, my voice flat. It's a confirmation of what I've suspected all along. She'll go to any length to save her own skin.

Sharon just smirks, unfazed. "A woman's gotta do what a woman's gotta do. Who knows? Maybe we'll be seeing each other again outside these walls before too long."

That's all I need to hear. The confirmation of her betrayal, her complete lack of remorse, her willingness to sell out her allies and her own child... it all wraps up any lingering doubts about the kind of person she truly is. "Good luck with all that," I tell her, my tone dripping with disdain.

Sharon hurls a few choice words my way as I stand to leave, but they're insignificant and bounce off me. I've heard enough, seen enough. I nod to the woman in the booth next to ours, giving her the signal. Then, I simply walk away, leaving Sharon and her delusions behind.

As I'm about to exit the visitor's area, a sudden commotion erupts from the prisoner's side. A part of me wants to turn back, but I know exactly what's unfolding without needing to see it. A small grin spreads across my face as security alarms go off.

I reach the exit, allowing myself one quick glance at the mayhem before I leave. The guards are scrambling; their efforts focused on pulling the blonde woman I had briefly acknowledged earlier away from Sharon. She holds a shiv in her hand, tinged red with blood, and though I keep my expression neutral, there's a dark satisfaction in knowing that she's executed the plan—and Sharon—flawlessly.

The guard standing by the door, his face a mask of professional detachment, leans in as I pass. "You'd better get moving," he murmurs, his tone low but urgent. "Doesn't look good, you being here while all this goes down."

I nod, ready to leave the prison and its grim dealings behind. As I walk through the door, I can hear a guard's exclamation, "Jesus, she's dead!" The finality of those words, the closure they represent, only cause my grin to widen as I step farther away from the visitor's area.

Leaving the jail, what's just occurred doesn't burden me; instead, there's a sense of completion, of loose ends neatly tied up. Sharon's threats, her potential to unravel the peace and safety I've fought so hard to secure for Maura and our future child, are nullified in one swift, decisive act.

The world outside seems brighter, the air fresher, as I make my way back to the car.

Sliding into the plush confines of the back seat, the sense of a chapter closing washes over me as the vehicle glides away from the jail. My phone vibrates, a coded message lighting up the screen, a signal from one of the guards inside confirming the success of our meticulously laid plan.

Sharon Flanagan no longer exists; she's now an eradicated threat, ensuring the safety of my family's future.

Without hesitation, I draft a message to my financial manager, instructing the confidential confirmation of payment to the woman who carried out the deed. She's not going to see the outside world for a long time, but her actions have secured a substantial sum for her family. Two million dollars can change lives, even if she's paying a hefty price for it.

And no price is too high to pay to ensure the safety of the ones I love.

I settle comfortably into the plush seat, my thoughts turning to Maura. She's the heart of all my actions, the reason I've waged wars and brokered peace. But how will she react to the lengths I've gone to protect us? The morality of my world is a far cry from the one she envisions for our child.

The reality that I'll need to share the day's events with her looms over me, and feelings of dread and necessity take over. Maura's strength and resilience are qualities I've come to adore, but what I need to tell her is a whole different beast. The truth about how I've ensured our safety, about the darkness I've navigated to keep danger from our door is a burden I wish I could spare her.

Yet transparency has always been the foundation upon which we've built our relationship. It's not just about the physical safety of our family but about the trust and understanding between us. As the car turns onto the highway, leading me back to her, back to the life we're building together, I prepare myself for a conversation I never imagined we'd be having.

An hour later, the car pulls into the driveway. In the quiet sanctuary of my study, I pour myself a drink, the amber liquid a temporary solace for the trepidation brewing within me. The door opens slightly, and one of the staff, ever discreet, informs me that Maura has arrived home. I steel myself for the conversation ahead.

Maura enters, radiant, her pregnancy lending her an ethereal glow. In that moment, with the soft light illuminating her features, she's the embodiment of everything pure and good in my world. She begins excitedly, "Luk, the ultrasound was amazing! The baby is healthy and—"

I raise a hand, gently stopping her mid-sentence. "Maura, I apologize, but there's something I need to tell you before you go on," I say, cutting her off. "Something happened today. Part of me wants to keep it from you, but you've asked for honesty, and I promised I will always give it to you."

Confusion flickers across her beautiful face. "What are you talking about? What happened?"

Taking a deep breath, I let the truth spill out, raw and unembellished. "Sharon is dead. I arranged it," I confess, watching her closely for any sign of how deeply my words have struck.

Maura's reaction is a mixture of shock and disbelief. "You... *what*? Why would you... How could you?" The questions tumble out, each one reflecting the turmoil I've just thrust upon her.

I move closer, needing her to understand, to see the necessity behind my actions. "I did it to protect us, Maura. To ensure our family's safety. Sharon was a threat, not just to me, but to you and our child. She had the means to get herself out of jail, and I couldn't let that happen. She was going to come for you again, for all of us. I couldn't allow what she'd done to stand."

The room fills with tension, a tangible force that seems to press down on both of us. Maura's eyes search mine seeking answers, clarity, perhaps even remorse. "I know this is hard to accept," I continue, "and part of me hates the fact that she left me no other choice. But I need you to know, everything I do, every decision I make, is to protect what we have, what we're building together."

Maura continues to search my eyes for answers as the silence stretches between us, a chasm filled with unasked questions and unspoken answers.

CHAPTER 30

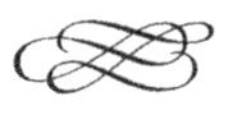

MAURA

"Are you... is this some kind of sick joke?" I ask Luk.

His face is serious, the look in his eyes grave. "No. It's no joke," he responds, his voice steady, quiet.

I have no choice but to believe him. He places his hands on my shoulders, a gesture both comforting and grounding. "What are you feeling?" he asks, his concern for my reaction clear. "Talk to me."

I'm torn, a whirlwind of emotions battling inside me. "I-I can't believe it," I finally manage to say. Suddenly, the reality of our life, of *my* life, the wife of a Bratva leader, settles in more than ever before. The world we occupy is complex and often brutal, and decisions like the one Luk has made are part of the fabric of our existence.

I look up at him, taking a deep breath. "Thank you for being honest with me," I say, and I mean it. Honesty has always been our foundation, the thing that's kept us strong amidst all the chaos. To my own surprise, there's a small, hidden part of me that feels tremendous relief, justice coming full circle.

"I'm surprised by how relieved I feel, actually," I admit, the words feeling strange even as I say them.

Luk's eyes search mine, looking for any sign of doubt or fear. "I know it's a lot to take in," he says, his voice gentle. "Please know that I didn't make this decision lightly."

"I know you didn't," I reply, feeling a renewed sense of partnership between us. "And I'm grateful for that. It's just a lot to process."

"Let's just focus on the future now," Luk says, wrapping his arms around me. "On us, on our baby. That's what truly matters."

"There's something I need to tell you, too," I admit hesitantly, drawing his full attention. Luk nods, his expression softening, signaling that he's all ears.

"It's about my father's estate," I continue, gathering my thoughts. In the meantime, I've named a close family friend as the executor. His name is Liam Gallagher, and he was like an uncle to me growing up. He's recently come back after being away for many years."

Luk's interest is piqued, a slight furrow forming between his brows. "Liam Gallagher? I remember the name. Where has he been?"

I take a deep breath. The next part is harder to explain: "It turns out Sharon had driven him away from the family through blackmail. She threatened him to ensure he wouldn't interfere with her deceitful plans." The bitterness in my voice surprises even me.

"So he's back now? To help manage the Flanagan legacy?"

"Yes," I confirm, feeling a flicker of hope. "He came back when Sharon went to jail. With Liam overseeing things, the Flanagan legacy will be preserved. Our neighborhoods will stay safe and continue to flourish, just like before." It's a piece of good news amidst the turmoil, a sign that not all is lost.

"And the other Irish families?" Luk asks, his strategic mind always looking at the bigger picture.

"They know to keep their distance now," I assure him, a sense of statement creeping into my voice. "Especially with the alliance between the Flanagans and the Bratva. It's a clear message that we're united, stronger together."

Luk nods, a small smile playing at the corners of his mouth. "That's good to hear. It sounds like you've got everything under control."

I laugh softly. "Yeah, with your help. But it's definitely a great start."

Luk's gaze softens, a silent question hanging in the air between us. "Do you want to continue to tell me about the baby now?" he asks gently.

I smile warmly as I say, "Our son is healthy, and he's growing as he should be, steady and strong, just like his father."

Tears form in Luk's eyes, a quiet expression of elation and pride. He leans in, planting a soft kiss on my forehead before picking me up and spinning me around. I laugh joyously as he exclaims, "We're going to have a son! I love you, Maura; I love you so much. Never forget that everything I do is for you and our baby boy."

The sincerity in his words wraps around me like a warm safety blanket. "I know that. And I love you, too," I tell him. We stand in front of the fire, holding one another. The flames dancing and crackling in the hearth are a soothing presence.

Despite the horror of recent events and the shock of learning about Sharon's death, I find myself accepting the complexities of our lives entangled with the Bratva. I'm feeling good—good about being married to a man like Luk—a man whose love and loyalty know no bounds, who would, and does, go to any lengths to protect the ones he loves.

As I step out of the car and into the sunshine of Bridgeport the following morning, I can't help but smile. It's like stepping back into a chapter of my life that I thought I had closed forever, but I'm glad I didn't. The neighborhood is buzzing, alive with the familiar hustle and bustle that I grew up with.

There's a new energy in the air, a sense of renewal and hope that's been absent for too long. It's clear Liam's been busy since taking the reins of the Flanagan family, and his efforts to revitalize our community are already bearing fruit.

I take a moment to breathe it all in—the sights, the sounds, the very essence of home. It's comforting and grounding and reminds me of simpler times before life became so complicated. But in my moment of reflection, something feels off. As I wander the streets of my childhood, I can't shake the sensation that I'm not alone.

I glance around, trying to spot the source of my unease, but nothing seems out of place. My bodyguards are discreetly following me, and knowing they're there should ease my mind, but the feeling of being watched persists, nagging at the edges of my consciousness.

I quicken my pace slightly, trying to dismiss the creeping sense of paranoia. Maybe it's just the aftermath of everything that's happened; my senses are still on high alert. Or perhaps it's a reminder that in our world, being cautious is always a necessity, not a choice.

Despite the unsettling feeling, I push forward, determined not to let it dampen my spirits. Bridgeport, with all its flaws and beauty, is a part of who I am. And as I walk the streets, surrounded by the echoes of my past and the promise of a brighter future, I'm reminded of just how far I've come.

The neighborhood, now under Liam's care, is slowly but surely reclaiming its identity, its strength. And I, alongside Luk, am building something new, something beautiful. The thought brings a smile to my face, a sense of pride and belonging that overshadows any fear or doubt.

Slipping into St. Brigid's Church, the familiar scent of incense and polished wood greets me. Father McCarry spots me from across the nave, his face lighting up with a warm, welcoming smile.

"Maura! It's so good to see you back and in good health," he exclaims as he makes his way over, his voice echoing slightly in the spacious church. "And I hear congratulations are in order? You're expecting a little one, yes?" His eyes twinkle with genuine joy, and I can't help but return his smile.

"Thank you, Father. You've heard correctly, and we're very excited," I reply, my hand instinctively moving to rest on my belly. But beneath the pleasantries, an underlying tension remains. Something about being in the church—perhaps the peacefulness of it, the sense of shelter it provides—makes me want to open up, to seek counsel.

"Father, could we speak alone?" I ask quietly.

"Of course, Maura. Let's step into my office for some privacy," he suggests, leading the way.

Once seated, I gather my courage, taking a deep breath before diving into what's been weighing on my heart. "Father, there's something I've been struggling with about my relationship with Luk," I start, my voice a bit shaky.

"Yes?"

"You're aware of the life he leads as it's much like the life many around here do," I begin.

Father McCarry nods, his hands steepling under his chin. "I think I know where this is going," he states.

"Yes, I suppose you do," I reply.

Before I can go any further, Father McCarry continues. "Maura, I can't say that I agree with the way some..." he pauses, "...businessmen approach their dealings, but I can say that if you are truly repentant, you can be forgiven."

I feel almost instant relief as I know Luk's decisions are not made without careful thought and never without regard for how they will affect the people around them.

"And what does it say of me to love a man who sometimes has to make those difficult choices?" I ask for my own sake.

Father McCarry sits back and smiles. "Maura, I've known you since you were born. I baptized you myself. I know your heart is a good one. I also know that you are not responsible for your husband's decisions any more than you were responsible for your father's. You, my dear, are your own woman, and the love you give to others is a reflection of the love God gives to you. Do not be troubled."

His words lift a weight off my shoulders, a burden I hadn't fully realized I was carrying until that moment. The guilt and uncertainty fade away, replaced by a newfound confidence in the love Luk and I share.

"Thank you, Father," I say, my voice filled with gratitude. "You've given me a much-needed sense of peace."

He offers a gentle nod, reaffirming his role as a guide and confidante: "I'm always here to help, Maura. Remember, love is the greatest commandment of all."

As I step out of the church, my personal security squad is there, as always, giving me the nod that it's time to roll out. As we head to the car, though, that weird prickle on the back of my neck returns—like someone's watching me.

I sneak a peek over my shoulder, but again, there's nothing but the regular Bridgeport buzz.

I try to shake off the heebie-jeebies, reminding myself I'm about as safe as it gets with my crew around. Besides, after speaking with Father McCarry, I'm feeling pretty invincible.

I hop into the car, and one of the guards shuts the door, a solid, secure sound. That feeling of being watched is still there, but it's taken a back seat to the excitement of getting home to Luk.

CHAPTER 31

MAURA

In the lush calm of the garden, I sit with Elena and Lily, sipping tea while basking in the delightful vibes of a golden afternoon. It feels like one of those snapshots of time you wish you could just freeze.

"We've been brainstorming names for the little guy," I say, giving my tea a lazy stir. "Got any ideas?"

Lily, eyes lighting up, throws in, "How about Jonas? I've always thought that was a cute name."

Elena snorts, amused, "Not bad. But knowing Luk, he'll probably want something with a bit of a badass vibe."

We all crack up, picturing Luk's face upon hearing our cute, gentle suggestions. It's the kind of laughter that makes your sides ache, the kind that comes from deep within when you're with your people.

Curious, I ask, "What about you two? Have you ever considered diving into motherhood? Maybe someday?"

Lily nods, a dreamy look on her face. "Yeah, if Mr. Right ever decides to show up. I do find myself fantasizing about having my own little family, though, regardless of whether he does or not. There are so many options today that would allow that to become a reality."

Elena's response to my question, however, is quite different from Lily's. She bursts out laughing, almost spilling her tea. "Me? Please. I'm swamped with trying to keep this family's heads above water. I can hardly fit in a date, let alone think about kids."

I nudge Elena playfully. "Don't close your heart. Love's sneaky—it shows up when you least expect it, and suddenly, you find yourself making room for it."

Elena rolls her eyes, but there's a smile behind them. "Okay, okay. I'll keep an open mind. But only because you make it look so good."

Lily adds, "Seriously, Elena. Love could be just around the next corner, waiting to surprise you."

Our laughter fills the air again, weaving through the afternoon's soft light and the shadows it creates. Our talk drifts from dreams to dares in the kind of heart-to-heart talk that stitches souls together.

Lily checks her watch. "All right, break time's over. We have salmon for dinner tonight, so don't spoil your appetites."

"Wouldn't dream of it," Elena says.

As Lily excuses herself, a shadow of concern crosses my face, pulling me away from the serene moment.

Elena, always the observant one, nudges me, her voice low and warm. "What's up? You've seemed off since we sat down."

I let out a sigh, brushing a strand of hair behind my ear. "I know it sounds crazy, but I can't shake the feeling that I'm being watched. It's probably nothing, right? Just residual effects from everything that's happened."

Elena's expression turns serious, her brow furrowing. "Maura, in our world, 'probably nothing' can mean a whole lot of something. But with Sharon gone and the Bratva's grip tighter than ever, who would dare?"

"I know, but..." I trail off, the unease staying with me.

Elena nods understandingly. "Listen, there's always someone looking to stir the pot, especially when they think the top dog might have a weak spot. But you know Luk, he's always three steps ahead."

Her words are meant to comfort me, but the knot in my stomach tightens. "I should tell Luk, shouldn't I?"

"Absolutely," Elena agrees with a nod. "If there's something to it, he'll find out what's going on and deal with it. And if it's nothing, then at least you'll have peace of mind."

She's right, as usual. "Thanks. I just hate adding more to his plate."

Elena smiles, placing a reassuring hand over mine. "Dealing with shadows is part of the job description for him. Besides, he'd want to know if something's bothering you. You are his number one priority, no matter what may already be on his plate. It's always better to be safe than sorry."

Elena's curiosity shifts, her eyes lighting up with a new interest. "So, how's the pregnancy going? How are you feeling?"

I can't help but beam, my hand automatically cradling my growing stomach. "Honestly, it's amazing. I was scared at first, but now, I love it more than I thought possible. Feeling him moving around in there, it's like a little miracle."

Just as our conversation deepens, Elena's phone buzzes on the table between us, breaking the moment. She glances at it, her expression turning back to business. "Ah, it's a message from Grigori. Bratva stuff; you know how it is."

I nod, understanding all too well the demands of the Bratva side of our lives. "Of course."

Elena looks up at me after reading the message, a smile returning to her face. "Hey, let's go grab lunch in the city tomorrow, just us girls. What do you say?"

"I say that sounds wonderful," I reply, genuinely excited at the prospect of some normalcy.

Elena stands to leave, promising to text me the details of the following day's lunch plans. Left alone with my thoughts, I am forced to realize how my life has taken so many unexpected turns in such a short period of time, but sitting there, in the serenity of the garden, I wouldn't change a thing.

My mind wanders to the blessing I received from Father McCarry. A warm feeling of acceptance and understanding envelops me. It's given me a new perspective on my relationship with Luk.

Lost in thought, a sudden vibration from my own phone pulls me back to reality. It's a text from Luk.

Need to see you.

Those four simple words send a thrill through me.

I hurry through the sprawling mansion, my steps quick and light. I can't help but smile and throw hellos to the staff as I pass.

The moment I step into our bedroom, I'm hit with a massive wave of desire. He stands by the window, the afternoon sun framing his ridiculously handsome features. He's wearing a suit that fits him perfectly, highlighting his broad chest and shoulders and every lean muscle in between. I can't help but want to skip the pleasantries and dive right in. Just the sight of him makes my pussy clench, and my panties are immediately soaked.

"What's up?" I ask, trying to sound casual and not like I'm mentally drooling over him. But who am I kidding? I've been head over heels for this man from day one, not just for the power he wields so effortlessly but for the softness he shows only to me.

He turns from the window. "How are you feeling?" he asks. I melt at the question because, despite everything, his first thought is always my well-being.

"Good," I say with a grin. "The morning sickness is hit or miss, but I'm hanging in there. How are you?"

He smiles at me, one that's only meant for me, and says, "I've been trying to work, but it's been difficult because I can't stop thinking about you."

I step closer, reaching out to touch the lapel of his suit. "Is that so?" I tease, my tone low and sultry. "And here I thought you were all about business during the day."

He reaches for my hand, bringing it to his lips in a gesture so filled with love that it swells my heart to near bursting. "With you," he whispers against my skin, his eyes never leaving mine, "it's always personal."

Everything else just fades away. The luxury around us, the weight of our roles, the endless responsibilities—it all just disappears.

He leans in closer, his voice a soft caress in the silence of our room. "You know," he begins, his eyes glowing with a mixture of pride and something deeper, more intimate, "this pregnancy... it's brought out even more beauty in you, something I didn't even know was possible. You're radiant."

His hand finds its way to my belly bump, and a surge of love floods through me at the contact. It's more than just a gesture; it's a connection, a shared moment between the three of us. I lean into his touch, cherishing the warmth of his palm.

Our eyes lock, and without another word, we kiss, deep and passionate, our souls mingling. The kiss is a testament to everything we are, everything we've been through, and everything we've yet to become.

But as things start to heat up, I pull back slightly, my heart hammering against my ribs. He looks at me, concern etching his handsome features. "What's wrong?" he asks, his voice laced with worry.

I take a deep breath, my nerves dancing under my skin. "I've been thinking," I begin, the words tumbling out in a nervous rush. "There's something I want to try. Remember the gifts you gave me a while back?"

The change in his expression is immediate. His eyes darken, a grin spreading across his face, one that says he's been hoping I'd come around to this idea.

He doesn't need to say anything; his grin says it all. He's been waiting for me to embrace this part of our relationship, to explore this facet of our connection together.

"Do you know where they are?" I ask.

He nods slowly, stepping over to one of the dressers and opening the top drawer.

"I'm sorry for the intrusion, but I took it out of your room after that night. I figured you had enough to deal with, and we'd revisit the matter when the time was right."

He turns slowly, the leather collar in one hand, the nipple clamps in the other. The sight of him standing before me, those tools of pleasure in his grasp, gets me so damn wet that I can hardly think straight.

With measured steps, he approaches the bed. My eyes are locked on the tools.

"How do we use them?"

"Let me show you. First, we decide which to start with. Ladies' choice."

My eyes flick back and forth between the clamps and the collar. I'm excited, more excited than I've been in a long time.

"The collar. Seems like it's a little more straightforward."

"It certainly can be. But there's an art to it."

As he comes over to me, my whole body is tingling. Slowly, carefully, he slips the leather collar around my neck. The material is cool and smooth, and as he locks it shut, I feel a sense of arousal. There's a small key, and he shows it to me before placing it in the drawer of the nightstand. The long, metal chain of the collar hangs from the side, pooling onto the bed.

A thoughtful expression crosses his face.

"What is it?" I ask.

"The sub/dom dynamic requires trust and care. And once those matters are established... well, you'll see how good it can get."

"I trust you," I say. "Totally."

"I know. But there's still the matter of the safe word."

"The safe word. Right."

"How about... Guinness."

I can't help but laugh. "Because I'm Irish."

One side of his mouth curls up in a sexy grin as he replies, "Either that or vodka."

"I've always been a tall-pint kind of woman."

"Guiness it is." He takes my chin into his hand and tilts my head up gently. "If anything happens that you're even a little unsure of, say the word, and we'll stop. Don't *ever* feel like you have to do anything you don't want to do. Just say the word. I want total comfort and consent."

His words accomplish exactly that. "Okay. Let's start."

Another smirk. He walks slowly from the bed and sits down in the chair in the corner of the room.

"Come."

He tugs the chain gently, enough to make it go taut. He uses just enough force to pull but not to hurt. I rise from the bed, and he slowly pulls the chain more and more, guiding me over to him.

Soon, I'm standing before him.

"Think of this leash as an extension of my hand. Where it guides you, you come. Understood?"

"Understood."

He seems to place extra emphasis on *coming* as if he knows precisely the effect he has on me.

"Let's begin."

He tugs the leash gently, guiding me toward his mouth. We kiss, his tongue finding mine, his free hand lifting my shirt and pulling down my pants. I help him, and soon, I'm nearly nude before him. His touch explores more of my body, caressing my breasts, teasing my hips, and venturing between my thighs just enough to send a fresh wave of arousal through me.

He tugs the chain again, this time guiding me to my knees.

"Open my pants."

I do so happily, undoing his leather belt, buckle, and zipper before reaching inside, taking hold of his cock, and pulling it out. My mouth waters as it always does at the sight of his manhood, long and thick, hard and dripping, just for me. I can't resist leaning forward and licking his head, tasting the salty bit of precum at the end.

"Someone's jumping the gun," he says with a smirk.

"Sorry. Couldn't help it."

He pulls the leash gently again, guiding me back to his cock.

"Since you've already shown such initiative," he adds with a wink.

Luk doesn't need to say another word. I go right back to work, extending my tongue and licking him up and down his length. God, he tastes so good, so perfect. His cock is like a treat, a delicious dessert I can't wait to devour. I alternate between licks and kisses, glancing up at him, loving the way he gazes down at me while I work.

When I've teased him enough, I open my mouth and take his head inside, lavishing it with my tongue as I suck. I glance up; my look is heavy with arousal. I move my lips down further, taking more and more of him into me.

Luk curls the rest of the leash's slack around his fist. When there's only a few inches left, his hand right by my head, he pulls down slowly, lowering me even further, more of his cock entering my mouth.

"See?" he asks. "A little guidance goes a long way."

It's hard to smile with my mouth so full, but his words nearly make me do it. To my surprise, deepthroating him isn't uncomfortable. It feels natural, even. Luk has merely pushed me past my limits to a place I'd deep down wanted to go.

He guides me off his cock, his length glistening. He stands.

"On the bed." The leash slackens.

I do as he says. Luk steps over to the bed, and I follow behind him, crawling. The sensation is strange but good. I feel like I'm his property, like he's truly claimed me.

Once at the bed, he guides me with the leash to my feet, then onto my back upon the bed.

"Spread your legs."

I do as he commands. Luk drops to his knees, covering my inner thighs with kisses before moving between them. He spreads my lips and begins to lick, slowly, with the flat part of his tongue. The pleasure is immediate, insistent, and incredible.

I run my hands through his thick, dark hair as he eats me, his tongue dancing over my clit, his fingers moving in and out. The pleasure builds and builds, and I come in no time.

I arch my back as he sends me over the edge, releasing a cry of total delight, Luk licking me through the orgasm. He stands up as it fades, slipping out of his clothes and pouncing onto me. Within moments, we're wrapped up in one another's arms, Luk's cock gliding into me with the ease it always does.

My eyes go wide as he fills me to the brim. The anticipation the leash provides brings things to a new level of intensity, and soon, he's pounding me hard, driving into me with powerful, deep thrusts. I open my eyes just a bit to watch his thick cock split me in two over and over, his muscles flexing with each drive.

"You're so goddam sexy," he growls.

"And this body?" He reaches down and grabs the fleshy part of my hip. "It's mine. All mine."

"Yes," I moan. "Yes, it is."

The words are a surrender, bringing both of us quickly to orgasm. Pleasure courses through me, a sensual eruption accompanied by Luk tensing up, his cock pulsing inside of me, draining his seed. I focus on our bodies and our breaths as we rise and fall together.

When our climaxes wane, he's at my side, holding me close. The sub/dom stuff... it's intense. And I know we've just scratched the surface. All the same, Luk understands the importance of making me feel loved and secure after it's done, making sure I know that the foundation of our experimentation is pure, sweet love based on trust.

He kisses my shoulder, placing his hand on my belly. "You're my everything, love."

I smile, nestling into his body.

"Don't ever forget that," he adds.

It's his final command of the evening, one I'm more than happy to obey.

CHAPTER 32

MAURA

One week later...

The crisp night air brushes against my skin as I step out of the car; the familiar sight of our home offers no comfort tonight. Every shadow seems to stretch longer, every sound a potential whisper of danger. I'm trying—really trying—to focus on the tiny life within me, the son whose grand entrance into the world we're so eagerly awaiting. But a relentless unease clings to me, a persistent shroud I can't seem to shake.

We're returning from having a nice dinner downtown. As much as I enjoy our date nights, part of me wanted nothing more than to stay home, where I know it's safe.

"I felt it again today," I mutter, leaning against Luk as we walk toward the front door. "It's like an evil pair of eyes on me at all times. I know it sounds silly, but..."

Luk's arm tightens around me, his presence always a solid reassurance. "It's not silly. Unfortunately, the life we lead causes us to make a lot of enemies. I'll have the guys sweep the area again, just to be sure."

"But it's been quiet, hasn't it?" I try to convince myself as much as him. "Since Sharon, since all that was sorted out?"

"It has," he agrees, pressing a kiss to the top of my head as we step inside. But the warmth of our home does little to ease the chill in my bones. "But we can't afford to be complacent, not with our little one on the way."

The baby kicks as if to remind me that he's there, thriving despite the shadows that continue to lurk. I place a hand on my belly, a smile tugging at my lips despite the fears. "He's active tonight." Luk smiles in response, that fierce, protective glint never leaving his eyes.

We settle into the living room, the fire crackling a soft, comforting hymn. "I can't help but feel that somehow Sharon is still a danger to us, even from the grave," I confess, the name tasting like poison on my tongue. "I know she's dead, but there were still a few left who were loyal to her. I'm scared they'll come after us to avenge her."

Luk's jaw tightens, his hand finding mine, squeezing gently. "I won't let anything happen to you or our baby. I promise you that. Anyone who thinks they can threaten my family will have to go through me first."

"I know," I whisper, leaning into his embrace, finding solace in his vow. "I just wish I could shake this feeling that we're being watched, hunted."

"We'll increase security," Luk decides, his voice firm. Tomorrow, I'll talk with the team. We plan to have a stronger detail on you at all times, no matter where you are."

As we sit there, the fire's glow illuminating our faces, I want to believe in his words, in the safety and love that surrounds us. If only I could shake this feeling...

The garden is quiet, almost eerily so, as I step outside for a breath of fresh air. Luk's still asleep; I didn't want to disturb him with my restless energy. The night envelops me, a blanket of stars overhead offering little in the way of comfort. My phone vibrates suddenly in my hand, a beacon of light in the darkness.

I unlock it, expecting a message from Elena or Lily, scolding me, stating that they spotted me in the garden and to get my butt back inside. What greets me instead is a message that chills me to the bone:

Do you think you could live happily ever after with your little family? Not if I have anything to say about it.

I look around the dark garden, half-expecting someone to emerge from the shadows. But there's nothing, just the whisper of the wind and the distant sounds of the city.

The garden, once a sanctuary of peace and solitude, suddenly feels like a trap. The darkness around me is oppressive, and the plants are menacing. I clutch my phone, the screen still displaying the chilling message, a direct threat illuminating the night.

I need to tell Luk, to warn him that Sharon's ghost is not just a shadow from our past but a present danger. My fingers tremble as I draft a quick message, but before I can hit send, the realization hits me like a cold wave: no service. My phone, usually so reliable, is now useless in my hand.

Panic sets in, a heavy, suffocating cloak. The notion that someone could engineer something as mundane yet as critical as cutting off my phone communication terrifies me. It's then, in the eerie silence of the night, that I feel it again, that prickle at the back of my neck, that undeniable sensation of being watched.

With every fiber of my being telling me to run, to scream, to do anything to escape this nightmare, I instead force myself to stand, refusing to let panic settle in. I begin the painstakingly slow journey back to the safety of the house. Each step feels like a mile, and the night air is thick with my fear.

Then, out of nowhere, a pair of hands, large and unyielding, clamp down on me, a cloth muffling my attempts to scream. Panic—raw and primal—courses through me. I fight, I thrash, but the grip only tightens, dragging me back into the darkness, away from the light of the house, away from Luk, away from safety.

A real-life nightmare is unfolding. The realization that I'm in the hands of an enemy, one who is here not just to threaten but to harm, causes a terror so profound, so all-consuming, that for a moment, the world blanks around me.

As the stranger drags me through the garden, his grip iron-clad and unyielding, I fight against him with everything I have. But it's like trying to move a mountain with sheer will; he's too strong, his body a statue of muscle and malice. I can sense his rage, can almost feel the storm within him.

"You took my brother from me, and for that, you'll suffer. Maybe I'll toss you off a roof like your husband did to Rory."

Confusion sets in for a quick moment as I struggle to see my assailant's eyes. The resemblance is unmistakable. The man detaining me is Connor Murphey, Rory's younger brother.

"My brother was my hero, and he's dead because of you," he continues, his words spoken with a chilling calmness. "So now, it's Luk's turn to suffer. He's going to know exactly what it's like to lose someone he loves."

The garden has become a sinister labyrinth, each turn a step further away from hope. As we round the next turn toward the exit, a new wave of panic runs through me—two of Luk's guards lay motionless on the ground, clearly taken down by Connor's hand.

He's getting closer to his goal of killing me, and the reality of the situation settles in with gut-wrenching clarity. Luk doesn't even know I'm missing yet. How can he save me when he doesn't know I need saving?

I can't rely on Luk now; I need to save myself. I twist and turn, trying with all my might to break free from Connor's iron grip, but my attempts are futile—he's much too strong, his hold unyielding. A cold dread settles over me as I realize the depth of his anger and his pain, a barely contained rage that promises nothing good.

Do you really think Luk will find you in time?" he hisses in my ear, his words dripping with venom. "Trust me, he won't."

The cold night air does nothing to ease the suffocating fear as Connor continues to taunt me, each word a twisted promise of pain and retribution. "I've decided I'm not going to drop you off a roof after all; that's too quick, too easy," he sneers, a cruel, amused smile forming. "I'm going to make sure you suffer first. And then, I'll send Luk a little video, a keepsake of sorts, reminding him of how he failed to save his wife and child."

My heart races, panic clawing at my throat as we reach a nondescript van parked away from the main road. The back doors are flung open, revealing two more armed men and another at the wheel, their faces masks of indifference to my plight.

Connor shoves me inside, the cold metal floor of the van greeting me sharply. He binds me quickly and efficiently as if he's done this a thousand times before. The doors slam shut with a finality that echoes in the hollow space, sealing my fate.

As the van starts to move, my hope dwindles. I'm at the mercy of a man consumed by vengeance; the horrors that await me are endless. The thought of Luk, of what this will do to him, is the greatest torment of all.

CHAPTER 33

LUK

"How the hell did this happen?"

I slam my palm against the wall, my voice a harsh growl echoing through the otherwise silent halls of the mansion. Anger and fear churn inside me, a lethal mix that threatens to boil over.

Elena matches my pace stride for stride, her usually calm face now etched with urgency. "We missed the jammer because it was low-key, running on a frequency we didn't expect. But the moment I saw the glitch in our system, I knew something was wrong. Fucker got the motion sensors, too."

Lev speaks next, his voice a low rumble. "We caught him on the security footage before he scrambled it. We ran facial recognition—it's Connor Murphy. Luk, that's Rory's brother."

We burst into the garage, a cavern of my achievements, but only one beast catches my eye now—the black Audi R8. It's more than just a car; it's a predator on wheels, sleek and powerful, every inch designed for speed and precision. I snatch the keys from the hook, my mind racing faster than any engine.

Elena and Lev are right behind me. "Gear up," I command. I had already instructed the guards to prepare the vehicle, our arsenal lying inside the trunk, a small army's worth of firepower—silenced pistols, submachine guns, and extra ammo—all for Connor, all for taking back what's mine.

I grab my weapon, and Elena and Lev follow suit. We're not just going to save Maura; we're going to end this nightmare once and for all.

I slam the trunk closed, the sound echoing throughout the garage. Sliding into the driver's seat, the leather feels cool and comfortable against my skin. Elena and Lev climb in; their facial expressions are tight and serious. I ignite the engine, and the car roars to life, a beast awakened.

"Let's move," I declare, my voice a deadly promise. I shift into gear, pulling out of the garage, the car cutting through the night. Every fiber of my being is focused on getting Maura back, no matter the cost. Connor has taken the most precious thing from me, and I won't rest until she's safe in my arms again.

The car slices through the night like a blade, its engine a growl that mirrors the retribution I seek. I race through the streets, downtown Chicago soon unfolding before us, a maze of light and shadow.

My focus narrows to one object just ahead—Connor's van. Elena had picked it up by hacking into traffic cameras, and we were able to narrow it down quickly and lose it even quicker.

Her brows furrow as her fingers fly across her tablet, working feverishly to track the faint signal from Maura's phone. "The jammer's messing everything up," she snaps, frustration evident. We're hanging on by a thread here."

Lev checks his weapon. "We need to end this tonight," he says, a deadly determination in his voice.

I push the accelerator harder, weaving through late-night traffic with a precision that comes from years of evading the law and rivals alike. "There it is," I announce, spotting the bulky shape of the van a few blocks ahead. The sight of it ignites a fury in me, a blazing fire that demands vengeance.

"We can't lose him again," I say, flooring the accelerator. The car responds instantly, closing the distance between us and the van within seconds.

Elena braces herself against the dashboard, her eyes locked on her tablet. "We've got one shot at this, Luk."

As we draw nearer to the van, Lev readies his weapon, his eyes cold and focused. "I'll take the front; you two cover the sides." Elena and I nod a silent agreement.

The van seems oblivious to our pursuit, and its driver is focused on the road ahead. It's a mistake I intend to capitalize on.

"Get ready," I say, my voice low. The car's engine roars louder as I prepare to make my move.

In a split second, I swing the car alongside the van, the suddenness of the maneuver catching Connor's men off guard. Lev rolls down his window, his weapon ready. Without a moment's hesitation, he fires, the sound of gunshots ripping through the night.

Chaos erupts. The van swerves, its driver thrown off by the unexpected assault.

I edge the car closer to the van, my eyes flicking between the road ahead and Connor, who's leaning out of the passenger's side, firing wildly at us. Bullets ping off the car's reinforced frame. "Careful," I say, acutely aware of the precious cargo inside.

Lev returns fire, steady and calm. I keep the car parallel, matching the van's speed, desperate to find an opening, any type of advantage. Out of the corner of my eye, I spot the barrel of a gun sneaking in between the front seats of the van. It's pointed straight at Connor's head. Confusion wars with opportunity in my mind, but there's no time to ponder the implications. I act on instinct, seizing the chance.

With a sharp turn of the wheel, I ram the car into the side of the van, metal screeching against metal, the impact jarring but calculated. The van veers off the road, scraping along the guardrail before coming to a stop. I brake hard, skidding to a stop a short distance away, my heart pounding with adrenaline.

Lev and Elena are already out of the car, weapons drawn, as I kick my door open and step out into the cool night air. My hand tightens around my gun, the weight of it both a burden and a comfort. "Maura!" I call out. "I'm here!"

We approach the van cautiously, aware of the potential for an ambush. But the silence that greets us is broken only by the sound of our footsteps crunching on the asphalt. Elena and Lev are flanking me, their guns at the ready. We are a silent, deadly trio, ready to take back what's ours.

The back door of the van is slightly ajar, a sliver of darkness that holds unknown danger. I slowly approach, with Lev covering me while Elena keeps watch in the front.

Without warning, the door kicks open, and time seems to slow down as Maura stands there, a vision of defiance and strength, the gun that had been menacingly pointed at Connor now firmly in her grasp. My heart leaps at the sight of her, unharmed and combative. She was fighting them, and I can't help but feel a tremendous amount of pride.

Before I can savor the moment for too long, two guards emerge from the shadows behind her, their intentions clear in their stance. "Maura, get down!" I shout, a command laced with fear for her safety. She doesn't hesitate, dropping to the ground and making herself small.

In the span of a heartbeat, Lev and Elena spring into action; their training and instincts are taking over. Shots ring out, quick and precise, the guards crumbling to the ground, the threat neutralized in the blink of an eye. Silence falls over us once more, save for the heavy breaths of those still standing.

Maura runs to me, a blur of motion fueled by adrenaline and relief. I catch her in my arms, holding her close. The warmth of her body against mine calms the cold dread that had settled in my heart. Her presence, solid and real, anchors me.

But even as we embrace, I know it's not over yet. Connor's threat still looms large, a shadow that has yet to be dispelled.

I pull back slightly, looking into her eyes, finding there the same fierce determination that matches my own. "We need to end this," I state, my tone firm and final, leaving no room for doubt. "Once and for all."

Rounding the side of the van, a quick glance confirms the driver is unconscious, slumped over the wheel, no longer a danger. It's Connor who commands my focus, the true threat lurking within the shadowed interior.

As I edge closer, Connor emerges from the van. He's armed, of course, the resignation in his stance doesn't quite mask the undercurrent of menace. "You might have won this round, Luk," he spits out, his voice a serrated edge of bitterness and hate. "But there's no peace at the top. You, of all people, should know that."

"Lucky for me, I'm built for war."

Connor's hand twitches, a subtle shift that signals his intent.

It's all I need.

Time slows, every sense heightened, as I make the split-second decision. My finger tightens on the trigger, and I take aim at Connor's forehead, precisely hitting my target.

It's over.

EPILOGUE I

MAURA

I step out of the car, my hand instinctively resting on my significantly rounded belly, feeling the lively kicks of my baby boy. It's a sensation that never ceases to amaze me, a constant reminder of the life Luk and I have created together. Elena hops out of the car after me.

"You look ready to pop, babe," she teases, a smirk playing on her lips.

"I *feel* ready to pop!" I tell her. I can't help but laugh, and she joins in, the sound echoing lightly in the cool air. "But we've still got a good week until the due date," I remind her, though part of me is hoping our little one might decide to make an early entrance into the world.

Our banter fades as we both turn to look up at the towering skyscraper before us. Elena's next words pull me back from my reverie.

"You know, a meeting like this could have easily been done on Zoom," she says, a hint of grumbling beneath her tone.

I shake my head, a smile on my lips. "There's nothing like an in-person meeting to get things moving," I counter. I've held this belief long before my pregnancy, and even more so now, as Luk and I navigate the waters of our expanding business and family life. "Besides, it's good to show them I'm not slowing down, not even a little."

Together, flanked by our two bodyguards, whose presence has become a reassuring constant in our lives, we make our way through the lobby. The interior is sleek and modern, and the air is tinged with the faint, crisp scent of luxury. People bustle about, their steps echoing against the marble floor, but there's a moment when it feels like the world pauses, taking in the sight of us.

We approach the bank of elevators, one of our bodyguards stepping forward to press the call button. The doors slide open with a soft whoosh, and we step inside.

Moments later, the doors slide open once again, and I waddle out, trying my best to look as tough and serious as my current state allows. Waiting for us in the conference room is Liam Gallagher, alongside a few other key figures in the Flanagan family. Liam, with his rugged charm, graying hair, and a smile that never goes away, rises to greet us. He's always had that elder statesman vibe, wisdom etched into every line on his face.

"Ah, Maura, it's good to see you," Liam says warmly, coming over to help me into my seat. I thank him, settling in with a bit of effort. "And congratulations."

As we get down to business, Liam doesn't hide his surprise. "I must admit, Maura, I didn't expect you to be wanting to take on a leadership role in the family."

"I'm surprised myself. But this operation was my father's life. To step away now, even with your exceptional leadership, Liam would feel like I'm abandoning his legacy."

Liam gives me a look of respect, his gaze understanding. "I'd be more than happy to step aside. Your father would've been proud to see you at the helm. However," he suggests thoughtfully, "perhaps it might be wise for you to work alongside me for a while. Learn the ropes, so to speak."

I'm about to agree when an unexpected pang of pain follows a sudden kick from my baby. I pause and take a deep breath, trying to brush it off as nothing, but it's enough to cause me a moment of concern. Elena catches my eye, her expression filled with worry.

"It's nothing," I whisper, hoping my voice sounds more convincing than I feel. "Just baby Ivanov making his presence known."

Liam doesn't seem to notice as he leans forward, his voice low and serious. "The Flanagan's have always been the top of the food chain, so to speak. But our alliance with the Bratva has made us nearly untouchable."

I nod, trying to focus on his words, but another sharp pain cuts through me. I bite my lip, determined not to show any weakness.

"However," Liam continues, "there's a new player in town—a Greek operation. They're ambitious and looking to carve out their own piece of the city. It's only a matter of time before they try to test us to see if they can shake our hold."

"That won't happen on our watch," I assert, trying to mask the discomfort that's growing harder to ignore. "We'll show them exactly why the Flanagans are not to be messed with."

Liam smiles approvingly. "That's the spirit. Your father had that same fire. But remember, it's not just about strength. It's about strategy and alliances. Knowing when to strike and when to hold back."

I'm about to respond when another spasm of pain hits me, stronger this time. My breath catches, and I realize something's wrong. Then, without warning, my water breaks, soaking the chair and floor beneath me.

Liam jumps up, his calm demeanor replaced by concern.

I'm in shock, my hand flying to my mouth.

I can't believe this is happening now, of all moments.

Elena is instantly by my side, her face etched with worry. "We need to get you to a hospital."

Liam is already on his phone, barking orders. "Pull the car around—now! We need to move quickly!"

I try to stand, supported by Elena and one of the bodyguards. "I was hoping for a less dramatic exit from this meeting, but I suppose this will have to do," I attempt to joke, though the fear and anticipation are enveloping me like a shroud.

Liam escorts us to the elevator, his phone still pressed to his ear. "We'll handle the Greek situation for now. You focus on bringing your little one safely into the world."

~

As the car speeds through the streets, I'm trying to find a comfortable position in the back seat, desperate to focus on anything but the intensifying contractions.

"You're doing great, Maura," Elena reassures me, squeezing my hand. "Just hang in there."

I manage a nod, relief taking over when I see the hospital looming ahead like a beacon, and before I know it, I'm being whisked into a wheelchair and through the bustling corridors.

I can hear Elena on her phone. "Luk, she's in labor. Get here as fast as you can."

I'm barely aware of the nurses and the flurry of activity as I'm taken into the delivery room. The pain is all-consuming now, each contraction sharper and closer than the last.

"You're doing great, Maura. The baby's coming soon," one of the nurses tells me, her voice calm in the hail of pain and fear.

"Already?" I gasp, the reality of the moment crashing over me. "I can't believe it's happening so fast! My husband isn't here yet!"

"Just focus on breathing," Elena coaches me, her presence a constant comfort. "Luk will be here any minute now."

The thought of Luk arriving in time for the birth of our child gives me a new surge of strength, and I cling to it, riding each wave of pain with determination.

The delivery room is a flurry of activity. A team of professionals moves with practiced ease as they prepare for the baby's birth.

Luk's arrival is heralded by his deep, reassuring voice, cutting through the fog of pain and fear. His presence immediately calms me. He's by my side in minutes, his hands finding mine, our gazes locked on one another with an intensity that anchors me.

"You've got this, darling. I'm here," he says, his voice a lifeline.

The nurses guide me through the process as the doctor prepares for the baby's arrival. The pain is intense, a nonstop crescendo that threatens to consume me, but the thought of holding our baby gives me strength. I push with everything I have, a desperate effort to bring our child into the world.

After one final push that makes me think I might black out, there's a cry, the most beautiful sound I've ever heard. It echoes through the room like a ray of sunshine cutting through storm clouds. Luk cuts the cord, a symbolic gesture that marks the beginning of a new chapter in our lives. Our son is placed upon my chest, my arms instantly wrapping around him in a protective gesture, and the world narrows down to the tiny, perfect being cradled against me.

He's here—a beautiful, healthy boy. His wide and curious eyes meet mine, and at that moment, everything else literally fades away. The pain, the fear, the uncertainty—all of it is washed away by the overwhelming love that floods through me. Holding him, feeling his warmth and his heartbeat, I'm struck by a sense of completeness, of perfection, that I've never known before.

Luk's hand is steady on my shoulder, his presence a comforting weight. "We did it," I whisper, my voice choked with emotion. "He's perfect."

My husband's smile is all the response I need. Together, we've created something beautiful, something indestructible —our family.

The room fills with a new kind of energy as Luk carefully, almost reverently, takes Michael into his arms. The transformation is immediate and profound; the hard lines of his face soften, his usual intensity melting into something much softer, gentler. My heart swells seeing such tenderness from a man known for his strength and, at times, his ruthlessness.

"Look at him, Maura. He's incredible," Luk says, his voice full of awe and pride. The sight of this big, intimidating man holding our tiny son so delicately is enough to bring tears to my eyes. It's a side of Luk I've only seen glimpses of but never so fully, so purely.

He walks over, a careful guardian of our newborn, and gently places Michael back in my arms. He kisses me then, a soft, lingering touch that speaks volumes. "I love you," he whispers against my lips.

"I love you, too," I reply. Our eyes lock, and we share a moment of profound connection over the life we've created together.

The door then bursts open, admitting a parade of love and noise in the form of Lev, Yuri, Grigori, and Elena. Their faces are alight with excitement, each clamoring to get a look at Michael, to share in our joy.

"Ah, look at him! A heartbreaker already," Lev declares, his usual humor shining through.

Yuri, ever the stoic one, has a softness in his eyes that's rarely seen. "He's strong, that one. He will be a great man someday," he states with certainty.

Grigori, not to be outdone, edges closer. "Can I hold him next? Before he becomes a great man who breaks hearts?" Laughter fills the room, a light, joyful sound that wraps around us, binding us together in this moment of pure happiness. One by one, they take turns holding Michael, each offering their own blessings and predictions for his future.

It's chaotic, it's loud, and it's absolutely perfect. As I watch our family dote on Michael, I realize that this is what life is all about—love, family, and moments of pure joy that come when you least expect them. My son, in his first hours of life, has already brought us all closer together, his tiny presence a powerful reminder of what truly matters.

EPILOGUE II

LUK

Two years later...

Standing on the edge of the sprawling lawn, the mansion lit up like a beacon behind us; I can't help but feel a sense of pride swelling in my chest. It's Michael's second birthday, and the place is buzzing with energy and laughter. I'm trying to focus on the conversation I'm having with Grigori, but my gaze keeps drifting back to where my son is, his laughter the most captivating sound in the world.

"He's such a handsome boy," Grigori remarks, following my gaze for a moment before bringing the conversation back to the task at hand. "About the expansion, we've got the South Side nearly under control, and with the east looking to fall into place, we're set for a total city takeover."

I nod, the strategic part of my brain kicking in, but then Michael's laughter rings out again, pulling my attention away. Maura is there with him, looking radiant and so fiercely content that it warms me from the inside out.

"Yeah, the east will be a nice win," I say in a distracted manner, my eyes tracking my son as he stumbles into Maura's waiting arms. "We need to make sure the transition is smooth and minimize any disruptions."

Grigori follows my gaze again, a smirk playing on his lips. "Luk, for a man planning a city takeover, you sure are easily preoccupied."

I can't help but chuckle. "Can you blame me? Look at my boy." My tone softens, a rare occurrence that doesn't go unnoticed.

"Understandable. But back to business, we've also got to consider our new ventures. The shipping lines are looking promising, and with the right moves, we could easily monopolize the market in Chicago," Grigori continues, trying to steer the conversation back to our future prospects.

I force my attention back to him, knowing the importance of what we're discussing. "Right, the shipping lines. If we secure them, we'll be in complete control of the flow into the city. It's a critical move."

As much as I'm invested in our conversation, part of me is always with Michael, watching as he runs from one family member to another, each face lighting up with joy at his presence. It's moments like these that remind me why I do what I do. Why do I fight so hard? It's not just for power or control; it's for them—for Michael, for Maura, for the future I want to give them.

As Grigori and I delve deeper into the complexities of our ever-expanding empire, the conversation naturally drifts toward Maura. Her ascent within the Flanagan operations isn't just noticeable; it's downright impressive. We recount recent maneuvers she's orchestrated, each one more impressive than the last. Her ability to navigate the treacherous waters of our world with grace and a firm hand has both of us tipping our hats in respect.

"Her latest play with the docks," I say, admiration lacing my tone. "She not only secured a better rate but also established a new route that's cut delivery times in half. It's brilliant."

Grigori nods in agreement. "And let's not forget how she handled the West Side dispute. Without a single shot being fired, she turned potential rivals into allies. Your wife is a force to be reckoned with, Luk."

Just then, as if summoned by our praise, Maura approaches us. She's a vision, effortlessly blending the role of a doting mother and a formidable leader. She's chosen a flowing dress that hugs her in all the right places, its deep green hue complementing her fiery red hair, which cascades over her shoulders in soft waves. The dress, accentuated with subtle gold jewelry, highlights her strength and elegance. She wears her power as effortlessly as the smile on her lips.

"Talking shop on our boy's birthday, are we?" Maura teases, raising an eyebrow in mock disapproval, her eyes dancing with amusement.

Grinning sheepishly, I can't help but admire her all over again. "Guilty as charged though we were also singing your praises, love."

She shakes her head, a playful smirk playing on her lips. "As flattering as that sounds, you two promised. Today is for family, for Michael."

I nod, guilty as charged. "You're right, as always. Time to put business aside and celebrate our boy." The genuine joy of the day, the celebration of our son's birthday, pulls me back to what matters most.

Maura's expression softens as she glances between Grigori and me. "Grigori, would you mind giving us a moment? Luk and I need to discuss something privately."

With an understanding nod, Grigori excuses himself, leaving Maura and me alone. There's a shift in her demeanor, a seriousness that piques my curiosity. "Let's go inside," she suggests, her voice carrying an underlying note of importance.

We head into the house, the noise of the party fading behind us as we make our way to our bedroom—a sanctuary away from the complexities of our lives. Once inside, Maura turns to me, her expression one that I've come to recognize when she's about to broach something significant.

As I pull Maura close, feeling the tension in her body, I'm reminded of her strength, of how much she carries on her shoulders in doing what she does—not just in terms of our family and business but the weight of her own thoughts, responsibilities, and fears. The kiss I place on her forehead is one of reassurance, a silent promise that I'm always here, no matter the potential trouble.

The balcony offers a view of life in its purest form—laughter, chatter, and the innocence of children playing. It's a stark contrast and welcome change from the world Maura and I often navigate.

"What's on your mind?" I ask, my voice low, filled with concern. "If it's the business, you know you can step back.

There's nothing more important than you and Michael." My words are genuine, the well-being of my family always taking precedence over the empire we've built.

Maura shakes her head, her gaze fixed on the horizon. "It's not the business, Luk." There's hesitation in her voice, a rarity for her. She turns to face me, her eyes searching mine. "I know we hadn't planned on expanding our family just yet, but..." She pauses, taking a deep breath. "I'm pregnant."

For a moment, time stands still. Her words echo in my heart. I search her face, expecting to find fear, but instead, I'm met with vulnerability, a rare sight seen by my wife.

The thought of being upset never crosses my mind. Instead, a wave of unbridled joy crashes over me. "Pregnant?" The word feels like a blessing on my lips, a gift we hadn't expected but are so grateful to receive. Without hesitation, I wrap her in my arms, my heart swelling with emotion so potent it threatens to overwhelm me. "I'm thrilled, Maura. Truly."

Her body relaxes against mine, her relief palpable. Tears of happiness glisten in her eyes, mirroring my own. "Really?" she asks, as if unable to believe my reaction.

"Absolutely," I affirm, my hold on her tightening. There's nothing I want more than to grow our family with you." The words promise my unwavering support and love for her and our growing family.

At that moment, the happiness of our son's second birthday carrying on below, the future seems even brighter, filled with so many more possibilities, the promise of another new life about to grow.

We stand there on the balcony for a bit, holding one another and watching the party below. "Imagine, two little tykes giving us the runaround," she says, her voice filled with happiness and excitement.

I can't help but grin, feeling a swell of pride. "With you guiding them, they're going to conquer the world," I tell her, meaning every word.

"With *us* guiding them," she corrects me. "And with you protecting them, they'll never falter," she adds, her fingers finding mine, a touch that speaks volumes.

I place my other hand on her beautiful face, pulling her close, kissing her long and deep. "I promise to add more to that later. But right now, it's time for us to return to the party," I say, my voice laced with earnest. I've taken to my role of being a dad like a fish to water, something I never saw coming but now can't imagine being without.

We head downstairs, eager to return to our son's birthday celebration. Our bond feels as if it's become even stronger, a joyous secret we now share that adds a new layer to our relationship.

Hand in hand, we step back into the fray, the laughter and excitement of the party a stark contrast to the serenity of our bedroom. The sun is shining down on us, mirroring the brightness of our spirits.

As we mingle with our friends and family, a silent exchange occurs between us, a promise that no matter what comes our way, we will conquer it. We've got plans and dreams, and now another little one is on the way. It's a future filled with unknowns, but one thing's for sure—together, we're invincible.

The End

Made in the USA
Monee, IL
18 November 2024